Cameo is devasted over the shooting. She and Shook search Rebar's home for leads. When she finds Rebar's latest invention, they rally with Ricochet's dark horses and set out to find Rebar's body. What they find shocks them all.

Another trip to Pine Ridge exposes more than the truth about Feather Blue. The legend surrounding her comes full circle, creating troubled feelings in Cameo and Shook.

Missing bodies, unorthodox medicine practices, and a cast of compelling characters drive this tenth book in the series into the unknown.

Feather Blue
Copyright © 2024 Shiloh Love
ISBN: 978-1-4874-4059-6
Cover art by Martine Jardin

Published by eXtasy Books Inc

Look for us online at:
www.eXtasybooks.com

FEATHER BLUE
FEATHER BLUE 10

BY

SHILOH LOVE

CHAPTER ONE

Late Morning — Amarillo

Rebar struggled to open his eyes. They felt heavy and crusted from deep sleep. He tried to sit up, but someone had a hand on his chest, holding him down. Slowly, his vision cleared enough to see.

"Who are you and where am I?" His throat felt gravelly, and his voice sounded hoarse.

"Don't try to speak," a female voice said. "You are wounded. Save your strength.

A woman. A woman is holding me down. He mulled that over. *I must be in bad shape if I can't overpower a female.*

"Who are you?" he asked again.

She pressed a warm wet cloth on his bare chest. Her touch felt gentle, but it still hurt. "My name is Feather."

Sounds familiar, he thought, trying to recall where he'd heard it. He felt too drained to think.

"You've lost a lot of blood. But the bullet went straight through and exited your back. There is no damage to your internal organs."

"Bullet? Are you a nurse?" He looked up into the prettiest blue eyes.

"I'm a Medicine Woman. Hush now." She rubbed a thick paste over his wound.

"You said a bullet. Was I shot?"

She nodded. "They dropped you off here for the day and will be back tonight."

1

"Tonight?" He began to feel a little panicky. "Who?"

"Two wah-shee-chue. One with pale hair and the other black hair. I have never seen them."

"What is wasicu?" he asked.

"White man. I am Lakota."

Dread washed over him. "Did Malika send you?" He remembered Shook's story about Malika's mystical appearance at White Wolf's cabin.

The woman shook her head. "No. She is evil. She has kept me in this house for a long time."

"I'm confused." He sighed, then winced in pain.

"You talk much for an almost dead man," she said. "I cannot make you strong enough to escape if you won't shut up."

He closed his eyes and racked his brain. However, no amount of effort helped him remember what'd happened, or how he ended up here in this unfamiliar house with a stranger.

His short-term memory seemed blank. He couldn't even recall what he was doing before the so-called shooting. Was he in a battle with Ricochet? He remembered everything up to a certain point. He tried to fight the grogginess and think.

I was overly distraught while the movers hauled everything out. Chamber and I argued. I ordered a pizza, then worked in my den all night.

He recalled playing around with his inventions to improve the stability on Face Palm. He drifted in and out of consciousness as the Indian woman hovered over him. She supported his head and made him drink a bitter tea that made him cringe. After finishing the mugful, he laid back and began to feel very relaxed.

Great, she drugged me, he thought. *Malika is using her mystery powers and posing as another woman and holding me hostage until they come back to finish me off.* He fogged out.

When he came to, she was still there. He had no idea how long he'd slept.

"You're awake," she said softly. "That's a good sign."

He stared at her. "What time is it?"

"Around noon by the position of the sun. There are no clocks in this place."

"How long have I been here?" He turned his head and looked at his surroundings. Bare walls and floor, small windows near the ceiling, and minimal furniture. His gaze moved over her. Long black hair framed a lovely face. She was dressed in a blue and tan dress with fringes dangling from the sleeves.

"They brought you here at sunrise."

"Why are you here, in this shack?"

She pointed to a hoop with a net woven within the circle hanging over the door window. Feathers and beads dangled from the object.

"A dreamcatcher?"

"Yes. Malika's magic lives within the web design. I cannot escape."

"I don't understand."

"It's a long story that you are not up for. Rest. You can escape and perhaps find the one who can free me." She inspected his wound. "Would you do that for me in exchange for saving your life and helping you escape from them?"

"Can't you just come with me? I don't even know where we are."

"I cannot." She sighed.

"I'm afraid I won't get far in this condition," he told her sadly. "I feel weak. Must have lost too much blood."

"If you don't leave by nightfall, you may never escape. They have evil plans."

"What about you?" he asked, worried over her safety for helping him.

"Malika would never let them harm me. I am her energy source. She has weakened me over the years, drained my soul to increase her power."

"You mentioned one who can free you."

She nodded slowly. "Her name is Cameo. She is half Lakota but recently she joined in spirit to a man who is also half Lakota. Before she gave her heart to this man, Malika was able to torment and deceive her. She tried pulling them apart in a sacred dance, but Cameo's faith was strong. She drove Malika back and is now the only person able to defeat her power."

Rebar remembered that name, the name of the woman his memory could never erase. He also recalled Shook telling them about the dance. "You know Cameo?"

Tears glistened in Feather's eyes. "She is my daughter."

He wrinkled his brow. "Must be a different Cameo. The one I know is Malika's daughter and has a twin sister."

"They are *my* twins. Malika stole them from me and sold them to evil men. Then she imprisoned me in this white man's house to use me for her malevolent schemes."

"This is really confusing." He closed his eyes to think.

Nobody had mentioned that Malika was not the mother of Cameo and Camille. This woman surely was trying to trick him. All the weeks he'd spent with Cameo, and their intimate conversations, she'd told him all about Malika's sad story of how the General stole her babies. One thing he knew about Cameo, she was honest to a fault.

He didn't believe this woman's outrageous claims. He couldn't understand why she'd helped him live. He began to wonder what her agenda was. *Could she be Malika's sister?*

"Are you certain that you don't know the names of the men who brought me here?"

"I do not know them. I sensed they were filled with hate. Since you are an enemy to them, I thought perhaps you could help me," she told him.

Ah, so she does want something. He didn't say anything

further. He couldn't trust a woman who knew Malika and claimed to be Cameo's mother. Her story made no sense. He was especially skeptical over her theory that a simple Native American decoration could harness enough power to hold her prisoner here.

Currently, his fate looked bleak. Two men, maybe members of Ricochet, evidently had a serious enough grudge to shoot him then drop him off in this rundown house with a crazy woman. The possibility that he was having a PTSD setback whipped through his mind. He could very well be caught in a serious delusion.

He contemplated his options.

Noon—Denver

"Is it legal for us to be doing this?" Cameo asked Shook as they roamed around the interior of Rebar's Denver home.

"No," Shook replied with a short light laugh. "But we need to investigate what you saw. When we're undercover this deep, being the law means stepping beyond it."

She began to grasp why he'd been so cagy about getting involved with her. His entire life seemed top secret.

"There's no blood anywhere." She wrinkled perplexed brows. "You do believe me, don't you?" She slanted a dissecting look his way. "You don't think I was having a PTSD hallucination, do you?"

"I believe you, love. I'll admit that I wondered at first because of your history of PTSD. But once you calmed down, your thoughts were organized and clear."

She followed him around. "What are you hoping to find?"

"Traces of gun powder. A slug. Missed blood droplets. Anything that indicates a shooting. Looks like someone cleaned up thoroughly. But never thorough enough. I detected the faint smell of bleach, but if I got a forensics team in here, they'd still find traces. Unfortunately, without blowing my cover and the whole mission, I can't do that."

"If we don't have a search warrant, anything you discover won't be admissible in court, will it?"

"We're not calling the cops, so no court. We're doing this the Ricochet way. I wouldn't trust the president himself right now given Shade's relationship to the General."

The strength in his voice thrilled her. He was tough, cool, sexier than any man she'd ever met, and knew what he wanted.

"What about the Bureau? Do you need to notify them? Send in a report?"

He stood still and turned toward her. "Baby," he began with a patient look. "We're so deep undercover that most of the Feds don't even know who we are."

Cameo watched him scour the floor. She'd never seen him do his FBI thing. He looked so serious and intelligent. "Do you mind if I snoop in his den? He showed me all his tracking devices, files, computer stuff. I may be able to find something that'll help."

He looked up with a slight smile. "You go right ahead. I'm so lucky to have a perceptive, cool woman."

"I'm the lucky one but thank you for that. Some days I don't feel so cool."

He gave her a wink before she walked across the room to Rebar's den. Everything was in disarray when she entered his private office. Papers lay strewn all over the floor. Drawers had been opened and the contents dumped. She poked her head out the door.

"Someone was searching for something," she told Shook. "His office is trashed. They must've come back after I left."

Shook joined her. They waded through the mess. Cameo booted his computer up and sat in the office chair. Sitting there where she'd seen Rebar many times induced waves of grief. Knowing he was dead cut deep.

"Well, whoever was trying to hack his computer isn't tech savvy," she remarked. "Rebar's files are all intact." She tapped a few keys and entered his password to the file folder holding all the info about his latest invention, hoping he hadn't changed it. "Bingo," she muttered as all his info on Face Palm popped up on the screen. "This is what they were after." She felt around the edges of the monitor for the external device. "Yep. Just as I thought. Rebar buried himself in work yesterday. I knew he was troubled." She pulled the device from the port. "Can we take this?"

Shook looked at her in sheer amazement. "You're a bright lady. Did Rebar know you paid this close attention?"

"He never minded me in here with him while he worked. He trusted me."

"He better have. You took a beating to protect his Face Palm invention."

She held up a micro SDX card. "Everything about Face Palm is on this itty-bitty card. Unreal."

"I'm gonna have another look around out there," Shook told her.

"Okay. I'll finish going through his office to collect anything else we don't want to fall into the wrong hands. I wonder if I should wipe all his important stuff just in case they come back to try again. I can save it. I'm sure he has another external floating around in this mess."

He gave her an approving nod. "White Wolf was right. He told me to find my heart, that you were the first step toward answers of my vision quest."

Pride shone in his gorgeous black eyes, drawing a smile to her lips despite this grim task. She hated the sadness but loved working side-by-side with Shook. After she'd sifted through all the papers, Cameo accessed all his files from numerous storage drives and loaded them onto a five terabyte USB flash drive she found in a desk drawer. Once she had everything transferred from his computer to the drive, she cleared his desktop files and reset the hard drive to factory default. Fortunately, Rebar had top of the line equipment, and everything transferred very fast.

If Shade sent someone else in to retrieve what he hadn't been able to, there'd be nothing for anyone else to find. Cameo knew her way around a computer but had never felt the need to disclose her skills. No one had earned that level of trust from her yet, except maybe the irresistible hot-blooded man in the next room with steel willpower.

"Everything's clean," she said when reentering the main room. She found Shook kneeling on the floor meticulously digging at the wall with a small knife. "Find something?"

He didn't reply until he finished what he was doing. "Here it is." He stood and held out a metal slug between his thumb and forefinger. "I know a guy in forensics. I'll have him run the ballistics on this. I have no doubt it'll match Shade's gun if we ever get our hands on it, and Rebar's blood. Looks like a .45 caliber," he muttered.

"Is that bad?"

"Baby, at close range any bullet is bad." He pulled her into his arms and kissed the top of her head. "I'm sorry you have to go through this."

"I don't know how to feel. I had just gained closure and felt kind of peeved at him for still holding onto his dreams of Camille. Now he's gone. I wasn't going to approach him to say goodbye or anything. I feel a little guilty over that."

"I understand. But you carry no blame. He never reached out to you. Try to stay focused on the reality of the situation. It's easy to get caught up in remembering just the good times in a situation such as this and forget why you wanted to move on."

She clung into his embrace, resting her cheek against his chest. "You're right. I didn't have trouble with reality when I was here listening to him fight with Chamber and Shade. He could not let go of Camille and everyone knew it."

Shook eased back and brushed her cheek with the back of one hand. "You okay, darling?"

"Yeah." She nodded and sniffed back tears. "Are we ready to get out of here? Do you have what you need?"

He nodded. "Not a soul will ever know we were here. I need to give Rider and Stoke a call. They at least need to know. No way are we tackling this without them."

"You'll get no argument from me. I wish my stuff wasn't down in Dallas. I'd like to check out all the files I swiped."

"I know you're not gonna like this, but we have to return to Dallas. It's where I'm living at this time."

She sighed. "I thought I left Texas for good. Do you live there fulltime?"

"No, babe. I don't have a permanent residence because of my line of work. I haven't changed my address since I left home."

"You legally live with White Wolf?"

He shrugged and smiled. "According to the government. It's a good address for an undercover Fed."

"Don't you worry someone might attack him?"

"Attack my father?" His brows lifted. "By the time they got up the mountain and within range of his cabin, they'd be sorry. He has a private arsenal that'll thwart the most daring predator. I'd never wanna cross him."

"Oh . . . I had no idea. He seemed so tranquil."

"He is. But a man's gotta protect himself and his home."

Surprising herself, Cameo wasn't put off by the weaponry in this case. She'd let herself fall in love with an undercover agent. She had to be realistic in accepting his way of thinking and stop viewing anyone who carried a weapon as an enemy.

She was sure that Rider and Stoke would be heavily armed. The time had come for her to separate memories of the General's armaments from the good guys' firearms.

"Are you okay with all of this?" he asked gently. "This is my life until I retire."

"Yes," she replied without hesitation. "I'm in love with you. When I give my heart to someone, I accept everything about them. And I've only given my heart away twice."

He placed a tender kiss on her lips then gazed into her eyes. "You won't have to do it a third time. This is the first time I've let anyone pierce the walls around mine. Took me till I was fifty to find the right woman. You'd have to walk away to end this, but you seem very loyal once your mind is made up."

"I am. I've never broken up with anyone, which is why I avoided serious relationships until recently. And I was skittish about that first one."

"How are those skittish feelings now?" he boldly asked, typical Shook, straight up no chaser.

She slid both hands into his inky black hair and made solid eye contact. "Gone with you, baby. I've never felt more solid with a man. I worked out all my jitters before giving my heart away this time."

"Mm, my kimimila. I'm so in love with you."

She couldn't withhold a flirtatious smile, loving his Lakota pet name for her. "I'm looking forward to feeling the full extent of your love."

He nuzzled her ear. "I was ready last night in the shower. But the timing was really bad."

Quivers of excitement raced through her. She leaned into his embrace with a dreamy sigh. "My hot Lakota man, destiny will give us our perfect moment . . . soon I hope."

"We should go," he murmured in a husky whisper. "My self-control is waning being so close to you. And this is definitely not where I want our first time to take place."

"I agree." She reached up and kissed him then sighed with desire when he kissed her back with intense passion. "You're right," she said on an airy breath. "We better go."

Chapter Two

Sunset — Amarillo

By sunset Rebar felt a little stronger. The Indian woman had been tending his wound all day and making him drink the bitter tea.

"You must leave now," she insisted. "They will come for you soon. If you find Cameo, please . . . please tell her Feather Blue is alive. She will know what to do. I saw her in a vision quest last night."

Rebar cocked one brow skeptically. "You saw Cameo last night? Yet you haven't left this house in how long?"

"Forty years." Her expression became incredibly stoic.

"But you were with Cameo last night . . ."

"You speak folly like wah-shee-chue. You know nothing of our ways. And I don't have time to explain. If you find my daughter, tell her about me. She was in the vision with you. Her soulmate will interpret the vision for her."

"Soulmate? Has Cameo gone back to Rush?" His mind reeled at the thought. *Cameo has moved on. I've lost her. I missed my chance that day and now she's gone back to the bastard. She must've given up on me and went back to him.* He sighed despondently.

"I do not know the man's name, only that he danced with her, and they share the same faith," Feather told him.

Just the act of thinking exhausted him, driving home the realization of the severity of his situation. The only man he could recall with Cameo was Rush, and how she'd expressed doubt about staying with him. If only he'd thrown her a lifeline that day, they'd be together in his lodge instead of apart.

"Can you at least agree to find her and tell her? Cameo is in danger from these men. They seek something she has found. Will you do this?"

Rebar heard the seriousness in her voice, saw the heartbreak in her incredibly beautiful eyes. She was right. He was clueless about Native American ways. But he would at least relay her message to Cameo if he found her. It was the least he could do to repay this mysterious woman.

"Okay. I will tell Cameo about you if I find her. I can't guarantee that I'll find her, though. But I will try."

"Thank you." She handed him a small leather satchel. "Eat these herbs every hour. They will give you strength. I will find a way to stall the men so you can get as far away as possible."

"Where are we? I don't know in which direction I need to start walking."

"Somewhere in Texas," she replied. "I am not from this area. Malika brought me here when I was sixteen, and three months pregnant. And I have set no foot outside since. The moon crested on the seventh month of my seventeenth year the day my girls were born. We share the same birthday."

He calculated the years with her age. "You just turned fifty-seven this summer?"

She nodded. "What month is it now? I see through the window that the leaves are beginning their change. Is it the harvest season yet?"

"I believe so." He rubbed his temples. "My brain's still foggy but last I recall . . . September is only a few days away."

"Then yes. That is my age."

A sense of regret washed over him. "It will be two months since I broke up with Cameo."

"You didn't want her?"

"I was confused. Her twin sister, who I had known for a

year . . . never mind. It's a mess. Let's just say I made the biggest mistake of my life letting Cameo go."

Feather folded both arms across her chest with a dignified expression. "That is why you were in the vision with her, because you were her lover. I wondered why you were there."

"What's this vision you keep talking about?"

She ignored his question and walked into the small kitchenette. He began to wonder if she really was Cameo's mother. But that was so farfetched, he couldn't even wrap his mind around it. Cameo would never have lied. This woman was posing as an imposter, for whatever reasons, he didn't have a clue.

He braced his hands on the floor and pushed to his feet, then struggled into a standing position on shaky legs. He needed to get out of there and away from this strange woman.

"Can I ask you something before I leave?" He wobbled into the kitchen.

She turned and stared straight through him with those striking blue eyes. "What?"

"Why did you save my life?"

"Because they told me to," came her stark reply. "Without me, you would have bled out and died because the bullet did nick an artery. Now perhaps you can save mine."

"I'll try." He gave her a polite nod then shuffled toward the door, wishing he felt stronger.

No sooner did he reach for the knob when footsteps sounded outside. He heard someone approaching the door. Rebar glanced at Feather who shook her head sadly before walking back to the main room.

The door flew open. "Hey, welcome back to the land of the living, mate!" Chamber said as he and Shade swaggered into the house. "Looking good for a man on the brink of death."

Shade stared at Rebar for a minute then turned his eyes on Feather. "You'd be in trouble right now if Malika knew you were trying to help him escape," he told her. "Watch your step Medicine Woman."

Feather showed no emotion. She simply went about her tasks.

"Rebar . . ." Shade sighed. "What are we gonna do with you?"

Rebar stared at Shade. The sight of his black leather sport coat stirred a recollection. He vaguely remembered Shade pushing that jacket aside to reach behind him. Then he spotted it. Shade's .45 pistol. "You? You shot me?"

Shade laid a hand on his shoulder. "Don't go ballistic on me, boy. We both know you're in no shape to take me on today."

"Come back to finish me off?" Rebar scowled.

"Now you know that I've never failed a mission. Had I wanted you dead, I'd have put another bullet in you. Instead, we brought you here. We knew Feather would be able to stop the bleeding and help keep you alive."

"So what's this? Are you going to use some kind of sick torture tactic on me that you learned from your old man?" His memory began to clear.

"You look trashed, buddy. Have a seat." He gestured for Rebar to sit on a beige sofa. Shade plopped down beside him. "Seems to me that everyone's been jawing about my business."

"I haven't told them anything they didn't already know. Camille and Malika are your loose-lipped troublemakers."

"Yeah, yeah. I'll take care of them. But you, my friend, were going to tell Ricochet about Chamber. Now, is that any way to treat your best friend by putting a bullseye on his back?"

Rebar glanced at Chamber who stood silently beside Shade like a sentinel. "Nobody likes a snitch. You should know how I feel about them."

"I'll give you that." Shade nodded. "But, Rebar, what were

you thinking? Rush was never going to make you a real member of that pack. Those losers only wanted your techno skills. They used you to flush out my father. What kind of men harass an old retired General of his stature?"

"The kind who want justice." Rebar glared at him. "You know what that man did. And now you're sleeping with the woman who killed him?"

"You're only seeing the small picture. My father would rather die than be humiliated in court or prison."

"You think that justifies Malika killing him?"

"It was an act of mercy," Shade stated with no emotion.

"Wow... she got to you, too. She had the General wrapped, now she's got you around her little finger."

"Nobody controls me. I'm not here to explain myself to you. I'm here to offer you a choice."

Rebar scoffed then winced in pain. "Don't you mean an ultimatum?"

"See it as you want. But let's look at some facts. Everyone knows how you feel about Camille."

"Felt," Rebar corrected. "I feel nothing for her now."

"You never were a good liar." Shade laughed mockingly. "Chamber told me all about how you waffled between the twins. Let's stay on course here. Rush has one woman you love and Shook just took the other one."

"Shook?" Rebar didn't recall anything between Shook and Cameo. "She was with Rush. You're not making sense."

"Rush screwed up and Cameo took off... right into Shook's arms. Personally, I think she could've done better, like going back to you instead of settling for that freak. But it opened a door of opportunity for both of us."

Rebar's thoughts swam with confusion. *Cameo and Shook. How did that happen and where was I when it did?* He dropped his head in his hands.

"Snap out of it, soldier," Shade barked. "Don't go losing

your head over a woman. I've got a proposition for you."

Rebar lifted his head just far enough to look at Shade. "I'm all a flutter with anticipation. Can't you tell?"

Shade chuckled. "I always did like you. So, here's the deal. You come back home where ya belong, a member of my troop. Bring Talon and Kohl with you. I know they're your buddies and I like them, too. They'll follow you. And I'll give you something you've wanted a very long time."

"You don't have anything I want."

"Camille . . . lovely, sassy, muscle car manic Camille. You fell for her at first sight, chased Cameo when you thought she was Camille, broke up with Cameo when Camille said she wanted you . . . face it buddy, you never stopped loving her."

Rebar mulled over his words. Unfortunately, he'd made a valid point. He had fallen for Camille. He had chased her twin, thinking it was her. And he had dumped Cameo cold for a shot at Camille. He felt pathetic. "Let me guess. Camille pulled her seduction routine on Rush, too, and Cameo caught them. You sent your fiancée after another man? What's wrong with you?"

"No, I didn't send her. Camille doesn't like the arrangement I have with Malika, so she split. Now's your chance to be a hero again. Camille's floating around in Ricochet land because you blew her off when she tried to make amends. Do you really want Rush to have Camille after he stole Cameo right out from under you?" Shade taunted. "Has anyone in Ricochet mentioned moving you past probie status? Do they appreciate what you bring to the table?"

Rebar cast Chamber a cynical look. "Been doing some talking, huh?"

"Just looking out for you, mate." Chamber shrugged. "They haven't shown you any respect. And they moved in on both girls. Just ain't right, man."

"What makes you think Camille would leave Rush for

me?"

"Damn, Rebar. Give yourself some credit," Chamber growled. "You have a hell of a lot more to offer her than he does. And the two of you have a history. I doubt it would take much persuasion to win her back."

"Think about it," Shade added. "Wouldn't you love to take Camille away from that rebel biker who took advantage of your girl? Wouldn't it feel good to deliver karma to the prick?"

"I see what you're doing," Rebar said. "This is part of your war strategy against Ricochet. You want to use me as a pawn."

"No," Shade refuted. "You left us, remember? We want our troop back. All eight of us. And you'll have the woman of your dreams."

"Until you decide you want her back." Rebar scowled.

"It's not like that this time. I'm with Malika now. Camille threw her engagement ring at me and stormed out. I can't think of anyone better to scoop her up than you. She's always had a thing for you."

"And what if I say no?"

Shade sighed and leaned back with a frown. "Then you'll be our enemy. You're a smart guy. Who do you want as your allies? Your Marine comrades who've known and trusted you for years? Or these new dudes who treat you like you're invisible?"

"Why the hell did you shoot me?"

"To get your attention," Shade replied. "There was no getting through to you. When Chamber lost his mind, I was able to reason with him. But you're a hardhead. I had to get radical."

"What's it gonna be?" Chamber asked. "Us or them?"

"Why are you so bent on destroying them?" Rebar wanted to know.

The lines of Shade's face tightened. "They stuck their nose into my business and they're not gonna stop unless we make them. They should stick to what they do best, helping women and children, and leave the hard stuff to us."

Rebar stared at Chamber with a probing look. "What about you? Why'd you do what you did?"

"Payback," Chamber replied, appearing somewhat uneasy over being called out in front of his boss. "You wanna know why I've been a wanderer all these years? Do you?"

"Tell me," Rebar said, noting an uncharacteristic shift in Chamber's tone of voice.

"Years ago, right after I leveled up from probie status, I fell in love with a rescue. She was sweet and faithful, much like Cameo. And she loved me, too. But Rush was against it. He was all about rules back then, throwing his status as leader around. He sent me up north on another assignment. When I returned, she was gone. He told me dating rescues was forbidden, and he moved her away and changed her name. To this day, he won't tell me where he placed her or what her new identity is." Chamber's expression deepened with a mix of pain and rage. "Seems he modifies the rules as he goes, to suit his needs. That's why I continually roam. I keep hoping one day I'll find her."

"Wow . . . I had no idea. Why didn't you tell me? We've been friends for decades." Rebar began to see things differently.

Chamber shrugged. "You had enough trouble of your own when we found you. I didn't want you worrying over me. But when Cameo showed up, it reignited those emotions I buried, so I decided the time had come to make Rush pay. And I have the means . . . the same means you have, mate, to get back at him and maybe find my girl. Shade's troop is the only one with enough power to best Rush and his guys."

"He's right, Rebar. All the General's influence and contacts are now mine. And I'll stop at nothing to help those loyal to me." Shade shifted into a more casual position, resting one arm on the sofa back. "Here's the takeaway, buddy. You're brilliant but it takes more than technology to do what I can do. You picked the wrong team by joining forces with Rico-chet. And now Camille's running down the same path. Cham-ber jumped the gun and started his own plan without coming to me first. But as you can see, we worked it out. I value the men in my troop. I'm not entirely unreasonable when they make mistakes. However, I am a hard man. Can't change that."

"What about her?" Rebar glanced at Feather. "Why are you holding her prisoner?"

"We don't get involved with Indian affairs. She's Malika's problem."

"I don't know. This all seems extremely shady." Rebar's fo-cus shifted between the two men. He had a feeling that *no* was not an option here. Yet, how could he join forces with men who treated women this way?

Then there was Camille, floundering around among the ranks of Ricochet. If things didn't work out with Rush, she'd have no one left. The other members wanted nothing to do with her. And that was another problem. She had to be feeling edgy over the blatant rejection from every Ricochet member except Rush. How long would their leader go against them? He didn't seem capable of a serious commitment to a woman. It was only a matter of time before he gave Camille the boot to regain respect from his family again.

Rebar knew Cameo was out of his life for good now. She'd moved on with Shook, much to his surprise. But Shook was definitely a better man than Rush. He simply could not see a future for Camille with the man. The guy had no integrity. And nobody seemed to even know what their relationship status was. Only that she was staying with him out of desperation, and the pack resented her presence.

Chamber spoke up again with an urgency, unlike his typical casual demeanor. "Don't ya think it's time someone knocks Rush off his pedestal before he breaks Camille? She's hanging on by a thread."

Ricochet seemed dysfunctional and Rebar thrived on discipline. Chamber had made a few good points. He'd clearly been buzzing in Shade's ear all this time. *But how can I rejoin Shade's troop knowing what I know, and with Malika as his woman?*

"Hey," Shade said. "You don't have to change your lifestyle. Things can go back to the way they were before this Ricochet group rode onto the scene. Only this time, you'll have Camille in your lodge and your bed every night. You'll have everything you ever wanted."

"Just forget about this place," Chamber added. "Go back to Denver. Relax in your home. Be our tech guy and enjoy the peaceful life with the woman of your dreams. It's just that easy. Don't make this so hard, mate."

"Something tells me if I say no, I won't be walking out of here," Rebar said.

"We're not killers," Shade rebuffed. "But I will tell ya, if you return to those lowlifes, you'll put yourself in our crosshairs, if ya get my drift. War will rain down on Ricochet. We don't take betrayal lightly. Malika has it out for Shook and I'm not gonna let them get away with attacking my father. Be the hero you've always been, Rebar, come back to where you have a respected rank and rescue Camille in the process."

"Because if Camille doesn't get away from Rush, she'll go down with them," Chamber stated. "Can you live with yourself if Camille gets hurt because you refuse to step up and do the right thing? Rush will do the same thing to her he's done to every other woman who fell for him."

Rebar glanced at Feather. She shot him a fiery glare, then quickly looked away. As bad as he felt for her, he wasn't convinced by her outlandish story. She was an odd one for sure. Staying in this house for forty years without going insane seemed unlikely. He wasn't sure he wanted to step into Malika and Feather's drama over the twins. And he didn't believe that a common Native American decoration like a dreamcatcher possessed any power, especially enough to hold the woman prisoner.

Cameo had made her choice. He couldn't do anything about it. And sadly, she'd have to go up against Shade and Malika if she stayed with Shook. However, Camille was still vulnerable, and Rush couldn't be trusted at all. A difficult decision necessitated immediate attention.

Rebar felt he knew what he needed to do. Though he now abhorred Shade and everything he stood for, and he loathed Chamber's unwavering loyalty to the man, a beautiful woman had unknowingly become Shade's victim. If there was the slightest chance that Rebar could free Camille from Rush's selfishness and Shade's depravity, then he'd risk everything to save her. Even if doing so meant joining forces with them against Ricochet, saving Camille and having her as his own after loving her from afar for over a year would end his loneliness.

He understood now how Camille had been coerced by Shade and Malika into seducing him and trying to steal his tech secrets. No doubt, those two had made a mess of her head. They were a fearsome duo that he didn't want to cross again.

For a fleeting moment, he thought about Camille's nursing skills. He stole another glimpse at Feather who'd tended him all night. *Is it possible she's telling the truth? Could this woman be Camille's mother?*

"When do I get to see Camille?" he asked.

A satisfied grin softened Shade's tense expression. He handed Rebar his phone. "Call her. Tell her I shot you. She's a nurse, she hates me and adores you. I bet your life she'll jump in that fast car of hers and rush to your rescue."

"And if she doesn't?"

"Then I'll shoot ya again while she's on the phone with you. That'll light a fire under her ass for sure."

Rebar's brow shot up, but he kept his cool. "You sticking around till she shows?"

"No. Once I know she's on her way, Chamber and I are heading back to my place. Camille will be more than happy to take you home and nurse you back to health. If you call her now, she'll be on her way. It's a five-hour drive so time's a wastin'. You can be on your way back to that peaceful life you love by tomorrow, maybe sooner the way she drives." Shade chuckled. "Your choice."

Rebar accepted his phone with apprehension. "You're that sure she'll come, huh?"

"I'm betting *your* life on it."

He had to admit the strategy was good. Nobody would know he switched sides, so he'd be safe in that respect. Camille would have the ideal reason to leave without arousing suspicion from Rush. And upon hearing Rebar had been shot, Ricochet would realize war had begun, which would give them a heads up.

Giving Rush a little payback will be a nice bonus.

"We just want our troop back together," Chamber said, squatting on the floor next to him, both arms draped across his bent legs. "When Shade found out I brought Ricochet in to help you and Cameo, he was pissed as hell, man. I regained his trust by setting up the ambushes. Make the right choice . . . call Camille."

Rebar felt bad that his best friend lost the only woman he'd loved because of Rush. He knew that feeling. He couldn't deny he'd enjoy Camille as his own private nurse. She was a natural and had a unique way of comforting people when she wanted to,

His options appeared limited. He hoped Camille wasn't

too attached to Rush. He needed a nurse now more than ever.

CHAPTER THREE

After Midnight—Dallas

Shook grabbed their bags from his Harley and walked behind Cameo up the short flight of steps to his apartment. They'd ridden straight through from Denver to Dallas, anxious to examine the information obtained from Rebar's computer. They kicked off their boots at the door.

"I think I was holding onto you in my sleep some of the time," Cameo kidded as she dropped onto the sofa.

"Don't worry, I had hold of your hands. I'll never let you fall." He gave her a wink, then retrieved two bottles of soda from the fridge and handed her one.

She picked up the dual meaning in his sweetly spoken words. "I know you won't." Her gaze moved around his apartment as he roamed about inspecting his domain. Everything was incredibly neat and clean. "This place doesn't even look lived in."

"I move around constantly." He left the room and returned a few minutes later with a very elite laptop. "I learned at an early age to travel light so most of the places I rent are fully furnished. I've spent very little time in this one."

"That's a nice computer," she said while watching him set it up. "Nicer than mine."

He gave her a quirky look and laughed a little. "You sound surprised. I didn't know you were into high tech."

"There's a lot that people don't know about me. Until I get to know someone very well, basic info is enough. They don't need to know everything."

"I gathered you know your way around computers by the way you pulled the info off Rebar's system and wiped it clean."

"I paid attention. He enjoyed my company while he worked." She fought back the sadness over his death. "Let's see what he was up to all day before he got shot. He'd been in his den most of the day." She pulled the SDX card and flash drive from the zippered pouch of her leather bag.

Shook inserted the devices into ports. His system was lightning fast. All the folders popped up immediately. He swiped his own folders labeled *classified* off the touchscreen.

"For your eyes only, huh?" she teased over his subtle move.

An adorable grin touched his lips. "You don't want to see all my boring FBI stuff."

"I've never found anything about you boring, my love." She playfully nudged his shoulder with hers.

"Likewise." He draped an arm around her shoulders and kissed her neck. "Go ahead and do your thing. I love watching your mind at work."

She enjoyed his affection, which came so naturally from him. He'd thrown out many confusing vibes before finally opening his heart to her and letting her in. She knew she was a lucky woman to have won this man's love. She also knew this would be the last time she trusted any man enough to give her heart away. She felt good with him, solid. They had taken small steps toward each other, slowly building trust, and dissolving past issues before moving forward to love.

While Shook nibbled at her neck, she tried to focus on the computer screen. She waded through file after file of Rebar's notes, graphs, equations, and sets of codes, in search of the tracking screen. "This may take a while." She swept her hair back and off to one side.

"Mm, I missed that spot," he murmured against her skin. He nipped lightly then blazed a trail of kisses from her ear to the curve of her neck. "You smell incredible."

She reached back and curled one arm around his neck then sank back against the softness of the cushion. Her eyes were tired from staring at a screen, and her body was exhausted from a grueling ride. His silky kisses swept all her stress away. She surrendered to the much-needed relief, sliding her free hand into satiny layers of black hair.

He brought his other hand up alongside her face and slipped his long gentle fingers behind and just below her ear while continuing raining his delectable kisses on every bare spot he found. His lips glided lower. His hair caressed her cheek. She placed a deeply affectionate lingering kiss on the top of his head, basking in the feel and scent of his hair.

Shook lifted his head and gazed at her with captivating black eyes that smoldered with wild passion. The memory of him dancing around the fire, bare chested and painted according to his Native Culture tradition, whipped through her mind. He'd invited her into his world twice to share that visceral encounter. She'd felt one with him and all the elements of nature, an experience she'd never forget.

"You're remembering the dance . . ." he said in a low sensual purr.

"Yes . . . reading my mind again?" she asked breathlessly.

A slight smile touched his sexy lips. "I see the fire in your eyes."

They moved toward each other at the same time, meeting in the middle for a hot kiss laden with desire. His heavy sigh floated around her. She welcomed his tongue into her mouth as he kissed her deeply. The arm he had around her shoulders glided down her back to draw her tight against him. She tightened her hold in his hair, winding those inky strands around her fingers while pouring her intense feelings for him into their heady kiss.

Time faded, taking her worries with it as he lavished hot affection over her and into her. They kissed and caressed each other's upper bodies, spiraling further into one another's aura. His touch was delicate, skilled, and made her ache for him. All she tasted, smelled, heard, and felt was Shook. Nothing else mattered in this moment except him — them — and their deepening love.

"I want to make love to you," he whispered in the few seconds their lips were free.

She gazed into his eyes. "Lead the way, my gorgeous secret agent man."

He smiled adorably at her response then swept her into his arms and off the sofa. She kissed his neck as he carried her back down the hall to his bedroom. Gently, he laid her on the thick plush comforter on his bed.

She watched him peel the black sleeveless tee off his torso to reveal droolworthy washboard abs and a perfect hairless chest. He shucked his jeans, but she stopped him from removing the ultra-sexy Nike briefs.

"May I?" She sat up at the edge of the bed and looked up at his magnificent face.

Heat flashed in his eyes at her request. "Baby, baby . . ." He sucked in a sharp breath at her touch.

She'd longed to touch him since the first night he'd strolled from the hotel bathroom wearing nothing but his snug, sexy briefs. He wound his hands through her hair as she slid the smooth black underwear slowly down long muscled legs.

He stepped out of them as they hit the floor. She kissed his abs with softly parted lips, leaving a moist trail with her tongue. She began working her way down, wanting to please him, to taste him. However, he tenderly stopped her.

"Kimimila . . . our first time . . . I taste you first, my love," he told her in such a loving way that tears misted her eyes.

He eased her back down onto his bed. Strong, impressively sculpted arms pulled the leather riding pants from her body and tossed them aside.

She about lost her mind when he knelt at the edge of the bed and his hair brushed her thighs. By the time he let up, she was a quivering mess and burning out of control.

"Shook . . ." she breathed out his name. "Please . . ."

She scooted up on the bed as he crawled onto the luxurious soft blanket and balanced his weight over her. His long straight hair fell around his face in beautiful layers. He stared down at her, his eyes glassy and brimming with affection. She couldn't tear her gaze away. His long black lashes cast smoky shadows in his eyes adding to his already mysterious allure. He embodied his heritage in every way.

"I love you," he said in that idyllic moment of anticipation right before their bodies joined.

She stared up at him in awe. "I love you, too."

He joined his body with hers, filling her with hard masculinity. He satisfied every ache of longing, left no part of her untouched. Their bodies meshed together again and again until both were utterly spent. They collapsed in each other's arms as the first streaks of dawn squeezed through the window blinds.

He gathered her into his arms and pulled the blanket around them. "You are mine, wild butterfly." His voice was soft and thick with emotion.

She snuggled into his loving embrace. "That's all I ever want to be, my love."

"Destiny was kind to us last night," Shook said with a wink over breakfast he'd had delivered from the local café.

"Indeed, she was." Cameo smiled. Her cheeks still felt flushed, and joy coursed through her veins.

"I enjoyed you more than words can say. Tasting you,

touching you, being inside you . . . I never imagined making love could make me that high."

"Keep talking like that, hot stuff, and we'll never leave your apartment," she teased.

A mischievous grin made his eyes shimmer. "Don't forget. I'm accustomed to the outdoors. I look forward to exploring our love in many ways."

Cameo set her fork down and sighed dreamily. "I get completely lost in your eyes and the way you talk to me. I may never accomplish my goals at this rate."

"Don't worry, my sweet. I'll keep a healthy balance between work and play. Though for the first time in my life, I'm more interested in play." He flashed a beguiling smile.

"I trust you to keep us on track because my self-control goes right out the window when I'm near you."

"Then we should get back to that computer and see what we can find. I promise to behave." But his eyes said otherwise.

She wagged a finger at him. "What you say and what I see in your eyes do not agree."

He laughed a little. "Don't worry, babe. I'll be strong enough for both of us. But you cannot blame my eyes for lighting up when looking at my stunning woman."

She felt herself blush at his flattery. The change in his aura was remarkable. He'd always been so guarded. She loved seeing this softer side, and especially loved that they'd finally opened their hearts to each other. She felt privileged that he'd chosen her as his mate. Of all the women who'd probably thrown themselves at him, he'd chosen her.

"What are you thinking?" he asked.

"How grateful I am that you made me yours," she replied.

He skimmed a kiss along her cheek. "That goes both ways."

They cleared the table together before retreating to the living room to resume their work. Hopefully she'd make better progress today after a blissful night of sleep and ecstasy.

She settled on the couch and continued her search through Rebar's files. Shook sat beside her.

"What's this?" He pointed to a popup.

"I don't know. It wasn't there last night. Maybe I finally unlocked the right file."

"What are you searching for?"

"Anything that might give us clues. Security footage. Tracking. It seems that his security system was disabled for the past few days. I wonder if he was in the process of installing a new system and Chamber knew about it. He could've told Shade, and they seized the brief window of no cameras to get him."

"I'm impressed. You think like a Fed. Are you sure you're not a secret agent?" he asked with a lilt of tease in his voice.

"Oh no. No, no, no. I work with animals and land. I'm not cut out for this kind of work. I just want to nail Shade for what he did. Rebar deserves justice."

Shook pointed to the popup again. "What are these purple dots?"

"Omigosh. Face Palm. Remember the tracking he used in Raton?"

"Yeah."

"This was it. He connected his cellphone somehow to monitor the movement." She leaned toward the screen for a closer look. "These aren't moving. But they should give a readout." She pulled to mind the many times she'd watched Rebar and shared his excitement over this. "I have a photographic memory." She closed her eyes to get a visual. "Okay . . ." She opened her eyes and looked at the keyboard then typed in a sequence she'd seen Rebar use.

"There it is!" Shook exclaimed then gave her an enthralled look. "You are brilliant."

"Nooo . . . just good at remembering things."

"And modest," he added. "You could definitely work in Central Intelligence. But I know, animals and plants. I'm still awestruck, though."

"I think I can connect this to my phone so we don't lose the blips. I remember Rebar telling Talon and Kohl they'd have to call him and relay them manually if the signal dropped." She focused hard, then tapped a set of codes into the Face Palm app. "There. We should jot that location down just in case my phone loses the connection. But if it doesn't, we can track these blips."

"What do you make of it?" Shook asked. "Why would Rebar's tracking be active now?"

"He was in his den all day before Shade shot him. I bet he was working on Face Palm. He was trying to stabilize the medium to last longer than seven days. There's only one reason Face Palm would be active now." She fought back the sadness trying to cloud her mind. "Rebar was probably testing it on himself that day."

"So when Shade and Chamber took his body, they had no idea he was wearing a tracking device."

"And knowing Rebar, he probably had it all over his hands. I bet these blips will lead us straight to his body." She became suddenly sad and whisked tears from her cheeks. "That sounds awful. We have to track his body . . ."

Compassion glistened in his eyes. "I'm sorry, babe. I know it hurts. But at least we'll gain closure and evidence. Give him a proper burial. He's a decorated war hero."

"Do you know this address?" She showed him her phone.

"I do." His expression fell.

"What? What is it?" She felt a lump of fear in her gut.

"Amarillo," he replied. "Same road where we saw those vacant houses."

"The General's human trafficking shacks?"

Shook nodded.

"Oh no." She tried not to cry. "Not sure I can return to that hellhole."

"Those must've been the houses in my vision. White Wolf was right. He said you were the first step in understanding my vision." He touched her cheek. "You don't have to come. Stay here and keep the doors locked. I can do this for you."

"I appreciate your offer. But I need to go. I need to have closure." She leaned against him.

He drew her into a protective hug. "I only offered in case you can't do this. I prefer you at my side."

"I have to face it. I feel like something is leading me. Maybe Rebar's spirit is reaching out from Heaven to help us find his body so he can move on. Maybe he's trapped between worlds until justice is served. I believe there's more than beyond our physical existence, even if many don't."

"I do," he said softly. "We'll figure it out," he reassured her. "Do you have everything you need from my laptop?"

"Yes. There's another matter we've overlooked, though."

"What's that, baby?" He pulled back to look at her.

"My car. It's still in a parking garage in Denver."

"We did forget about that. Do you want to get your car before following Rebar's tracking?"

"That would set us back quite a bit. It's a twelve-hour drive one way. I'm not up to a marathon run without sleep. We'd be looking at thirty, thirty-six hours minimum." She paused for thought. "No. My car will have to wait. I hope it's safe in that garage. I'm not sure how much longer Face Palm will stay active. How far are we from Amarillo?"

"Five hours give or take depending on traffic. If we leave now, we'll be there before dark for sure," he told her.

She drew a calming breath and exhaled. "Let's do this. I'm terrified of what we'll find. But we have no choice."

"Whatever we face, I can handle. Don't be afraid to lean on me, sweetheart." He placed a soft, lingering kiss on her lips.

"Thank you for being such a rock and so cool through all this." She wound her arms around him in a sincere hug.

"Hey," he said in his naturally soft-spoken way. "I see and feel how painful this is for you. Just because you moved on doesn't mean you quit caring, and I love that about you, your compassionate heart. Rebar made a huge mistake, but all the guys liked him. We'll get Shade one way or another. I need to give Rider and Stoke a call. How about you get ready to ride in the meantime, okay, babe?" He gazed into her eyes while caressing her cheek.

"Okay. I'll pull myself together and pack up."

"I'll have Rider and Stoke meet us in Amarillo. Then we'll ride to the exact location together."

"It'll be nice to see them again. Do they know about us?" She wondered how his closest friends would react.

"They were hoping. Last time I spoke with Rider, he was hopeful we'd hook up."

"He was huh?" She smiled.

"Yep. Last thing he said was, *get the girl this time.*"

"And that you did."

He looked her over with those *make love to me eyes.* "Maybe destiny will be good to us again soon." He gave her a wink before she sashayed to the bedroom to gather her things.

CHAPTER FOUR

Noon — Amarillo

Rebar fingered the phone, still somewhat hesitant.
"We haven't got all day," Shade pushed.

Right there, Rebar made up his mind and dialed Camille's number. To his relief, she answered right away.

"Hey, Camille. It's Rebar."

"Put it on speaker," Shade growled and nudged him with the pistol.

"Rebar?" She sounded shocked. "Why are you calling me? Are you looking for Cameo? She's not here."

"I know she's not," he said. "She's riding around with Shook somewhere."

"Really? Wow. I haven't seen or heard from her in a while. She was furious with me and took off. I kind of sensed he was sweet on her back in Amarillo."

"Seems your twin is more like you than we thought," Chamber interjected. "She's on a third brother now, too."

"Shut up!" Camille huffed. "Where are you, Rebar?"

Rebar glared at Chamber but did his best to focus on the phone call. "Speaking of Amarillo . . . I'm stuck there right now. Your fiancé drove to my house, put a bullet in me, then dropped me off in some ghetto housing area. I need your help."

Shade chuckled in the background. "Come get your boytoy, Camille, before I permanently render him useless."

"Oh my gosh. I'm so sorry Rebar. I didn't mean to bring

35

trouble into your life. Is anyone taking care of you?"

"There's an Indian woman here. She's been tending the wound and making me drink strange brew."

"Malika?" Anger rose in Camille's voice.

"No, not that lunatic. The woman here now is one I've never seen before. She seems a bit eccentric . . ." He lowered his voice. "She talks crazy. But she did keep me alive so far."

"I don't know anything about Native American culture. Their rituals scare me. What's the address, hon? I'll come get you and take you home."

"You're not angry with me?"

"Not anymore. Shade makes you look like a saint. Besides, you had a right to go off on me that day in Amarillo. I was being a bitch."

"What about Rush? Will he let you come?"

Camille scoffed. "I'm done with letting men dictate my actions. All his friends hate me. The tension here is thick and I haven't been able to drive my car since he locked it in his garage. He doesn't trust me at all. Won't let me go anywhere without him. Feels like I went from one control freak to another."

"Hey . . . you didn't feel that way in the bayou," Shade piped up.

"I wasn't in my right mind, Shade," she retorted. "I've wised up recently. Finding my fiancé . . . make that ex-fiancé in bed with my witchy mother was a badly needed wake-up call. So back off."

"You sound different," Rebar noted.

"Been through a lot." She sighed. "Tired of this war between Shade and Ricochet."

"You and me both," he agreed.

"Really?"

"Yeah. I just wanna go home, Camille, and resume my peaceful life."

"That sure sounds good."

"I've got plenty of room in that big lodge of mine. You're welcome to hang out with me as long as you want."

"This is your golden buzzer moment, Camille. What's it gonna be?" Shade taunted. "That pathetic loser Rush or the boy genius here you've wanted all along?"

Chamber laughed.

She hesitated. The line went silent. For a moment he thought he'd pushed too soon.

Then she said, "I would love that, Rebar . . . if you're sure it won't cause trouble for you."

"I'm alone, Camille. Just me rambling around in that empty house. I'd enjoy the company. And . . . I could really use a nurse."

"Well, I could never deny a request like that." Her voice carried a hint of tease. "Enable your location and send me a text. I'll be there tomorrow."

"Thanks, kitten. I really appreciate this." He sighed with relief. "Can't wait to go home."

"It'll be nice. Like old times," she said. "Not like the last time when Shade sent me up, but like when we used to sit on the porch and talk for hours."

"Aw, now see that? All I had to do was bring him down to your level, Camille. Now you two lovebirds can coo together," Shade added with a snarky edge.

Camille sighed loudly. "Someday your lucks gonna run out, Shade. And I won't be there to pick up the pieces again. At least Rebar appreciates me."

Rebar heard something in her voice he hadn't heard in a long time — resolve. She'd had enough, just like him, and was ready to put the past behind them. He almost felt relieved that he'd contacted her. Having the feeling of home in his life again would be great.

"I'll be on the road as early as possible, hon. Rest and drink lots of water. Stop drinking that Indian tea. You have no idea what she's putting in it. I'll get you out of there."

"Thank you," Rebar told her.

"See, that wasn't so hard, brainiac, was it?" Shade chortled then yanked the phone out of Rebar's hands and shoved it into his pocket. "Enough. We've got what we came for." He and Chamber stalked out of the shack slamming the door behind them so hard that the windows rattled.

"You're a fool." Feather approached and jarred him from thought. "Going back to those evil ones." She plunked another cup of tea on the table next to him.

"I had no choice." He looked up into her incredible blue eyes. "Besides, Camille is a Registered Nurse. She'll be better able to help me recover with modern medicine. No offense to your nature approach, and I'm sincerely grateful for your help. But I want to go home."

"You trust a woman who runs from man to man?" Feather stared him down, making him shrink beneath her very direct honest gaze.

"Camille had a troubled past. Then her fiancée cheated on her. She's trying to get back on her feet. She and I are kind of in the same place right now. We understand each other."

"Drink your tea." Feather folded both arms across her bosom and briskly walked away.

Rebar subtly slid the tea aside then pushed off the chair and made his way to an old model refrigerator where he found a bottled water. He hoped Camille would arrive soon.

"I will still try to tell Cameo about you," he said, hoping to ease her agitation.

"I don't believe you. Once Camille takes you home, you will forget me. I listened to what you said. You think I'm loco." She whipped around to face him. "You will soon find out the complete truth, Rebar."

"I'm not trying to upset you. I have a chance to get out of

here and help both of us. Would you rather Shade put another bullet in me?"

Her eyes narrowed as if contemplating the question. "In my culture, warriors do not bow to the enemy. They fight straight and true, with honor."

"Maybe that's why your people lost the wars. It takes strategy to win battles. Sometimes the mind is the most powerful weapon."

"You still speak like a fool. Thinking so highly of yourself. You know nothing. And you will continue to know nothing like a bird with its head in the sand."

His heart went out to her. Such a stunningly beautiful woman who engulfed in bitterness and probably suffering mental health issues. He didn't know her history and didn't feel competent enough to help her. Clearly, she was rooted in Native American culture, something he knew little about. He didn't even know how to converse with her and probably had offended this mysterious female every time he opened his mouth. Whatever her history with Shade and Malika, it felt way out of his comfort zone. Especially now while he was injured and weak.

A familiar rumble caught his attention. He'd know the sound of that car anywhere. He made his way to the back door and opened it.

Camille's white Shelby glistened brilliantly in the rays of the high Amarillo sun. She stepped from the car, looking a bit curvier than when he'd last seen her. *She always did like to eat,* he mused. *It's about time she put some meat on her bones.*

"Rebar!" She spotted him leaning against the door jamb. "You should be resting."

"I need to get up and move around once in a while."

She smiled warmly while hurrying along a flat dirt path to the door. "Let me take a look at you." She grabbed his hand and slowly led him to the sofa.

Feather stared at Camille intently. The Indian woman couldn't take her eyes off her. Rebar closed his eyes as Camille removed Feather's paste patch and cleansed the wound with disinfectant that she produced from a first aid kit she'd brought with her.

"I must admit, this woman did a good job tending the wound." She glanced at Feather and smiled. "Thank you for taking care of him. I'm a nurse. I'll take it from here."

Rebar leaned in close to Camille and whispered. "She thinks you and Camille are her twins. She was talking crazy."

Camille glanced at Feather and dipped one brow. "Crazy is right. Bad enough I found out Malika is my mother. I'm not ready for another nut to fall off the family tree."

Feather simply stared but remained silent.

Camille checked Rebar's vital signs and looked him over from head to toe. "You are one lucky fellow to be alive. That bullet was dangerously close to your heart. I could kill Shade for doing this to you." She applied a clean bandage to both wounds, front and back, with a deft touch.

"I've never been one of your patients," he jested. "Now I know how Shade felt."

She scowled. "I should've let him die in the swamp. Low down dirty pig. Only good thing that came out of that whole ordeal was meeting you." She finished patching him up then looked around. "Where's your shirt?"

"His shirt was beyond repair," Feather replied. "You're a medicine woman, too, like me."

"Uh . . . no disrespect, lady. I appreciate all you did for Rebar. But I have actual degrees in nursing. I use modern meds and treatments."

"The truth is not always easy to see," Feather stated. Her stoic expression masked any signs of maternal sentiment.

Camille studied her for a minute then looked at Rebar.

"Well, gorgeous, looks like you'll have to travel shirtless. I have a clean blanket in the car to drape over the seat so you don't stick to the leather in this heat." Camille glanced around the room while gathering her first aid items together. "Is anything else here yours?"

"No . . . nothing." He looked at Feather. The woman stared stone-faced, but fury blazed in those vivid blue eyes. He doubted he'd ever forget her. "I wish you well," he told her.

She turned her back to him.

"C'mon, hon. Let's get outta here and get you home. Maybe swing by a medical clinic?"

"I'll be fine," he told her. "You nursed Shade in the worst of conditions. I'm confident you can care for me at home."

She smiled and touched his face. "Thank you. I'll take good care of you this time. No more tricks." Before closing the door behind them, she looked at the woman. "Thanks again for taking care of him. If you give me your number, I'll get the proper address from you and send you a reward."

"I have no phone. No reward is necessary. It was nice to meet you . . . finally."

Camille nodded and grabbing Rebar's arm led him to her car. She shouldered a look back toward the shack but didn't say anything about Feather.

Rebar eased into the comfort of the leather seat. He couldn't recall the last time anything had felt this good. Hearing the engine growl to life beneath the shining white hood of her sixty-seven Shelby GT Mustang 500 felt like home. He missed his Gran Sport that got demolished in the twister.

"Get a new car yet?" Camille asked as she buckled up.

"No. Haven't had much luck finding one."

"I've got a seventy GSX sitting in my garage. Pulled it off an auction a few days before I caught Shade and Malika in bed. It's yours if ya want it, hon. I used my money to start my business so that Shade has no rights to it."

"You are the luckiest person I know in finding cars. Can't

believe you found another one. How long before it's road ready?" he asked, feeling excited about something for the first time in a while.

"Hm. Once your condition is stable, I'll get back to work. It'll feel good spending time in the garage again. But I won't go near Shade's house. I need to find a new locale for my garage."

"I'm sorry Shade hurt you."

She glanced over while driving. "Thanks. He really derailed by hooking up with Malika. My own mother yet. Good grief. What a mess. I had started back to school, ya know, to get my doctorate. Classes were in session only two weeks before I had to drop out. I can't think with all that's going on."

"I hear that. I've been trying to stabilize my newest invention. Had the tracking all over me the night Shade showed up." He thought back to that night and how he'd been testing Face Palm on himself for glitches. "I still don't know how long it stays in the host."

"You'll get it figured out. Are you sure about me staying with you? I don't want Shade coming up and harassing you again."

"I'm sure," he replied. "Shade is all for us getting together it seems. I don't mean to sound harsh, but he made it clear he's with Malika and he wants you to move on."

"I see." She paused meditatively then added, "I'm good with that. He's been a jerk ever since you left. When was that, like four months ago?"

"Almost. I met Cameo the first week of May. I left Shade's troop when they regarded her like public enemy number one."

Camille sighed. "I was no better. I treated her horribly. Where is she now?"

"I don't know." He shrugged. "Last I heard she took off with Shook. They've been traveling up to Pine Ridge. Turns out that Shook's father is a full-blooded Lakota medicine man."

"Wow. I guess Cameo is embracing our Native American heritage."

"And you're not?"

"Not after what I've seen." Camille scoffed. "If Malika is any example of what Native American women are like, no thanks. I'd rather not know anything about the culture. Her Indian voodoo terrifies me."

"Yeah . . . she is scary. Although Feather helped me. But she's also into some weird Indian stuff. Called herself a Medicine Woman."

"Sounds like you and I are traveling the same path lately," she noted. "Alone and displaced."

"Well . . . not so much displaced. You may not want to live with me when I tell you the deal I had to accept."

"Oh?" Her brows lifted.

"Shade and Chamber persuaded me back to the troop. They said if I chose to stay loyal to Ricochet, I'd be their enemy. Actually, he said anyone loyal to Ricochet will go down with them. He's still planning revenge on them for going after his father."

"I was shocked when Rush told me about all that. Holy cow. Could our lives get any more complicated?" She laughed a little. "So what do you have to do now? Are you back to being one of Shade's *yes men*?"

"No. They said I can go home and live my peaceful life. Just stay away from Ricochet. And they want my tech skills. Not sure why since I've patented and sold almost all of my inventions. He seemed more upset that he lost me, Talon, and Kohl than losing our knowledge. He still lives in a military mindset. Loyal to the end. Comrades in arms don't abandon each other. Shade never left the war."

"He felt terribly hurt when you left. Then furious when

Talon, Kohl, and Chamber followed. He doesn't deserve your loyalty, though."

"I know. But nobody needs to know I've switched sides. I'll resume working from home, help Shade's team with technology when they need it, and stay out of the way." He looked over at her. "And hang out with you."

"I'm glad Shade moved on," she said, then turned those pretty blue eyes back toward him. "Because I'm pregnant, Rebar, and the baby isn't his."

His eyes widened. "Rush's?"

She shook her head and focused on the road. "No. I was pregnant before I was with him. I missed two periods . . . July's and August's. You and I were together the first week of July."

His mind did a fast backtrack. He glanced at her belly. It did seem slightly curvier than her typically flat abs. "Are you saying it's mine? What about Shade?"

"Shade hasn't touched me in months. I'm guessing he hooked up with Malika sooner than I or anyone realized."

Rebar thought back to a peculiar phone call he had with Shade months ago when Shade admitted that Malika turned him on. "But we were only together one night."

"That's all it took, hon. You must have strong swimmers."

"Weren't you using birth control?"

"No. I wanted a baby before I got too old. I kept hoping Shade would want me again. But it never happened and now I know why."

"Wow . . ." Rebar's mind reeled. "This is quite a shock."

"I can raise the baby on my own if you don't want it. I'll even take a paternity test. I'm not trying to trick you or anything." She looked over again as they waited for a traffic light to turn green. "But I want this baby, Rebar. Especially since it's yours. There's no other man I'd want more as a father to my child than you."

"So it's true. Everyone said you were pregnant but to Shade and that you were too far along for it to be mine."

"How'd they know? You're the first one I've told."

"Malika told Cameo."

"She must've been spying on me. Crazy witch. She couldn't even get the facts right. Not sure what she hoped to gain by telling Cameo. I'm getting a paternity test to prove it's not Shade's. I'm just starting to show as I head into my third month. I don't think it's obvious yet, do you?"

"Not at all," he replied. "I noticed you gained a little weight, but it looks good on you. I also noticed you sounded different on the phone, just like you do now, more like the woman I first met over a year ago."

"Hope that's a good thing."

He smiled. "It is. I gotta admit that when I first heard the rumor, I was worried it might be mine. At the time, it was the last thing I wanted to hear."

"Because you still had hope for Cameo?"

"Not so much that, but because of everything. We were worlds apart. Strange how everything can change in the blink of an eye."

She merged onto the interstate heading north. "Are you still hoping to get back together with Cameo?"

"No. One thing I learned about your sister is that she doesn't give second chances to a man who betrays her. There was a brief moment when I thought we may've been able to work things out. But I blew it. And honestly, I don't think it would've been the same. She's true to herself."

"That she is."

"I hope you're not offended. But I'm glad you're getting a paternity test. There's been a lot of talk and—"

"Say no more," she cut him off mid-sentence. "I completely understand. You have every reason to not trust me."

He reached for her free hand. "I want to trust you, kitten.

And once we have proof the baby is mine, there'll be no room for people to mess with my head."

"Are you saying you want to help raise our baby?" Hope tinged her voice.

"Of course. I never want to be like my old man and abandon his sons, send their mothers money to ease his conscience. If this child is mine, I plan on having a fulltime role in its life."

"Wow . . . I didn't expect that." She sighed in relief. "I thought you'd hit the roof and kick me to the curb."

"We were friends before we were lovers. How about we start there again? I enjoyed our friendship."

"I'd love that. But what if Cameo decides she wants you back?"

Rebar stared out the window at the lines zipping by on the road. "She won't. I'm glad she's not with Rush, though. Shook's a good man. And they're both half Lakota. If she's found her soulmate in him, I'll be happy for them."

"Me, too. While I don't share my sister's enthusiasm for our Indian bloodlines, I do hope she finds peace. I did her wrong. I caused the breakup with both her boyfriends. I'm a horrible sister."

Rebar laughed. "Yeah, you are. But she's forgiving. I bet one day the two of you will find a way to get along. Until then, try to stay out of trouble. And I'd really feel better if you move in with me, especially if you're carrying my child."

"You're still a sweetheart." She smiled.

"Ah." He waved her endearment off. "I'm curious, was Rush upset when you left?"

"I think he was relieved." She scoffed. "I think we both were. Now he can hang out with his buddies again. I thought we'd get along great with our mutual love for restoring cars and other common traits. But he was moody. And he didn't trust me at all. This war between Shade and Ricochet has messed with too many lives. I just want my stuff off Shade's property so I never have to see him again."

"Now that I'm technically back in Shade's good graces, there shouldn't be a problem with that. I'll speak with him. We'll work something out for you to relocate your business."

"There are no words to express my gratitude for your kindness. I don't deserve it." Her voice quivered. "I don't even deserve this precious baby but I'm so grateful, and I already love it."

Rebar studied her face and pondered their conversation as she drove. It felt good talking to her again. She seemed like her old self before all the craziness poured into their lives. They'd have ended up together sooner had Cameo not crossed his path. Camille would've run straight to him and not Rush the day she found her mother in bed with Shade.

He wondered why fate had taken the long way around in bringing him and Camille together. He'd loved her first. They'd always shared a connection. And now she was carrying his child.

CHAPTER FIVE

Early Evening — Amarillo

"We made great time." Shook guided his Harley down a dusty single lane road. "I'm glad we didn't hit any snags and made it here before dark. It'll be easier to narrow our search with some daylight left."

Cameo clung to Shook, looking warily around at the rows of houses she'd passed during her last visit to this place. She didn't think much traffic drove through here by the condition of the road. He handled his bike skillfully as he weaved around buckled pavement and patches of loose gravel.

"I've lost the tracking signal." She stared at her phone sadly. "There's no activity and the blips are gone."

"Good that we wrote that location down. Nothing like a dependable hard copy. We'll start there and see what we find." His confidence calmed her worry.

"How much farther?" She leaned her head against his leather jacket with her arms wrapped around his waist.

He glanced at the piece of paper that he'd stuck to one of the mirrors. "Should be at the end of this road. These are the rundown houses I saw in my vision. It feels like we're close."

"I hate this place. Can't believe we had to come back here."

He gave her hands a gentle squeeze. "The General's gone now, love. We won't stay longer than necessary. Rider and Stoke should be around here somewhere."

"There!" She pointed ahead to a small four-way intersection where two men with long dark hair waited on impressive

Harleys. The most time she'd spent with Ricochet's dark horses was at White Wolf's cabin. She liked Rider and Stoke. They had a great sense of humor, were quiet, strong, and private like Shook. She could see why he trusted them.

She had been surprised when Shook told her that Rider and Stoke were also undercover agents. The three made a fierce trio and a force to be reckoned with. She wondered how they'd approach Shade. Would they launch a sneak attack or grab him in the open? She supposed it would depend on Shade's actions and how much proof they had in order to arrest him.

"Hey, you're actually early," Rider teased as they pulled up beside him.

Stoke laughed. "I'm surprised you made it at all given the way your passenger is dressed. Halo, you rock black leather."

She smiled modestly, touched by his flattery. "Thank you. I seem to be living in it lately."

"We'll make a biker babe out of you yet," Rider added with a grin. "We gotta get you conditioned for rally runs with us and our ladies. Now that you're with our man Shook, I see Sturgis in the future."

"C'mon, guys." Shook laughed. "You're gonna scare her off and we just hooked up."

"No worries, Halo. We tease a lot, but we'll never push. Stoke and I are really happy you and Shook are together. He's waited a long time for the right woman."

"No pressure, huh?" She laughed softly. "I hope I measure up."

Shook laid a hand on her thigh. "You're way past measuring up, butterfly."

She kissed his neck. "I love your sweet talk, baby."

He turned his head far enough for a quick kiss. "I was worried it might sound cheesy. I'm a bit old school."

Leaning forward, she whispered playfully next to his ear,

"If last night was old school, you can take me back in time any day."

A roguish grin curved his lips. He gave her another peck on the lips before giving full attention to Rider and Stoke. They sat staring, amused expressions on their faces while waiting patiently.

Stoke rolled his eyes and chuckled. "Do the two of you need a few minutes alone before we ride on?"

"We're good," Shook replied with a light laugh. "Stop being an ass."

The guys laughed. She enjoyed their comradery. They appeared totally at ease with one another and more open without the others around.

"I have never seen you this happy," Rider told Shook.

"Thanks, mate." Shook handed him the piece of paper they'd written the address Face Palm had projected. "This is a start. Tracking went inactive on the way down. Hopefully we'll find a lead at this point."

"Can't believe Shade shot Rebar. The man is as cold-blooded as his father." Rider scowled. "Get rid of one devil and his demon son takes over."

"Once we find the body, we can haul him in," Shook said. "I'd lay money down that the slug I dug out of the wall matches Shade's forty-five."

"What a bastard," Stoke said. "Wonder what his motive was."

"The million-dollar question." Shook sighed. "Seems extreme. Just because Rebar left Shade's troop? By the way they ransacked his office, seems they want control of his inventions."

"But we have them," Cameo piped in. "I cleaned Rebar's computer."

Stoke arched a brow. "Shook told us how brilliant you are with a computer. We're impressed. Not only are you beautiful, but also intelligent, courageous, and kickass. You're gonna fit in just fine with us, girl."

"I hope so. I haven't made any other friends since moving to America," she admitted, feeling embarrassed by the fact.

"No worries, darlin'. You just didn't meet the right people until now. You'll get on great with Shannon and Starr."

"Your girlfriends?" she asked.

"Yeah. Shannon is mine and Starr is Rider's woman," Stoke told her.

"Do they have motorcycles, too?"

"Nah. They ride with us. They're cool, though," he replied, then glanced at the sky. "We should get moving before it gets dark."

The guys kicked their bikes into gear and eased onto the road. Shook led out. Cameo watched the houses roll by as they rumbled down the beaten road. They were single story, brown frame houses sitting on tiny lots of brown grass and weeds. A few minutes later they arrived at a cul-de-sac. Shook slowly cruised around the circle then chose a driveway to park in.

"Why this one?" she asked quietly.

He cut the engine. "There's a dreamcatcher in the door window."

"Wow . . . you're observant."

"I saw one in my vision."

Rider and Stoke parked beside them. "We'll cover the back," Rider said. They dismounted and slipped silently around the back of the small rickety house.

"You can wait here, babe," Shook told her, tenderness in his voice. "It might be nasty inside."

"I'm coming with you. I'm not squeamish. I have to know."

He nodded. "Stay behind me then."

"Okay." She walked in his shadow as they crept toward the front door. He pulled a nine-millimeter handgun from a side holster concealed inside his leather jacket.

At the door, he stood off to the side and gently moved her behind him with one arm. He rapped lightly on the door. Nobody answered so he knocked again. Again, no response. He tried the knob, but it was locked. She watched him contemplate his next move.

He pounded on the door harder this time. "Anyone in there?"

Cameo thought she heard footsteps, however no one came to the door. Shook pulled a small black rectangular pouch from an inside pocket. He removed a slim metal tool and picked the lock. Though the knob now turned freely, the door still would not open.

"I really don't want to shoot my way in," he muttered.

A chill trickled up her arms, prickling the tiny hairs. Her gaze was drawn toward the window. She stared at the dreamcatcher with its feathers dangling off beaded rawhide strips.

Rider and Stoke rounded the corner from around back. "There's no rear entrance. None. Not even a basement door or window back there." A troubled expression beset his face. "You know I'm not easily spooked but this place gives me the creeps," Stoke said and Rider nodded.

Shook looked from one to the other, visibly thinking. He racked the slide on his gun. "Stand back, love."

She stepped away to wait with Rider and Stoke. Two shots rang out and echoed in the ghost-like neighborhood. Though the properties were all ramshackle and neglected, the land it all stood on had to be worth a fortune. She wondered if the General had left everything to Shade. If so, Malika had targeted a very wealthy man with powerful contacts as her lover.

"Okay . . ." Shook backed away from the house. "Now I'm slightly uneasy. I hit that latch pointblank. The door won't budge."

Cameo took a couple steps forward, mesmerized by the

dreamcatcher. Black and white feathers waved back and forth as if floating on a breeze, yet they were inside the house.

"Baby, stop." Shook grabbed her hand.

"It's okay," she muttered. "The dreamcatcher . . . there was one in the motel window the night of the tornadoes that night on our way to Pine Ridge."

"Malika's magic," Shook said in an ominous tone. "We should leave this place."

"No . . ." She moved closer, tilting her head as the feathers drew her into their dance. "That's what she wants. She placed it there to keep us out or maybe . . . someone in."

"You're right. I saw one in my vision. We're definitely at the right house. But why can't we get in?" Shook wondered aloud. "It's you." He turned her toward him. "White Wolf told me that you're the first step toward the rest of the vision. That you have answers and information if placed in the wrong hands would put many in danger."

"Face Palm," she said. "If Shade and Malika get hold of Rebar's inventions, they'd gain a terrifying level of power. He's dead now. I'm not sure what the patent laws are . . ."

He gazed at her in sheer awe. "Your intuition is almost supernatural. Lakota Medicine runs strong in you."

"Malika hung the dreamcatcher there to hide something." Sadness consumed her. "Rebar's body." She dabbed tears from her eyes. "I'm sorry. I shouldn't be crying over him."

Shook pulled her into a soothing hug. "It's okay to feel. You cared about him."

She pulled her emotions back under control. "Thank you. I'm okay." Turning back toward the house, she marched up to the door, somehow knowing what to do. "Something inside this house is calling me. Malika's woven spell has no power over my God." She flattened her palm against the window, closed her eyes and bowed her head. *Yeshua please come. Bind whatever evil lurks here.* She began to softly sing an ancient hymn, her very favorite called *Amazing Grace*.

As she neared the last stanza of the song, emotion deluged her. Tears streamed down her cheeks upon feeling the Holy Spirit. Cracks in the window formed beneath her hand and veined out in a circle. She opened her eyes, wiped her tears with her other hand, then gently pushed on the door.

The hinge squeaked open.

"I have no words to describe what I just saw," Shook said in quiet reverence.

"Incredible," Rider murmured.

Stoke nodded in agreement. "You sure own your code name, Halo."

Cameo stepped aside, trembling. "I'll go in last if you don't mind."

Shook gave her a quick reassuring kiss. "You're amazing." He sidestepped through the doorway with his gun ready.

Stoke and Rider edged in with him, their weapons drawn. Cameo splayed a hand across her face and peeked through her fingers while following them in. The fragrance of herbs rose above the musty smell inside. She looked around cautiously, afraid of what she'd see. Then she caught whiff of a familiar scent.

"He's here," she whispered to Shook. "I smell his cologne."

Shook gave her a curious look but didn't dispute her keen senses. She wondered what he was thinking of her peculiar behavior, but she remained quiet as they began searching the house, their guard on high alert. He stooped down to inspect stains on the unpolished wooden floor.

"Blood." He looked up at her.

Stoke and Rider moved from room to room with impressive stealth. Shook waited in the kitchen area with Cameo.

"No body," Stoke told him when they returned. "But someone is living here. The bathroom sink and shower are wet. There's a damp towel hanging on a hook."

Cameo lowered her hand and wandered around the kitchen. She opened the outdated refrigerator. "Food. Looks like stew." She closed the door. "Dried fruit, rice, cornmeal," she rattled off things she saw in a cupboard. "Wow, someone likes herbs. This is what I smelled." She stared at a shelf full of various herbs and spices then lifted one of the jars to her nose. "Hm, this reminds me of White Wolf's cabin." She held it under Shook's nose.

"Nettle Goldenrod," he told her. "Natural detox tea."

"Here's a jar of salve. Do you think Malika's using Native American remedies in her spells?"

Shook furrowed his brows. "Not likely. I don't know much about her type of magic, but I'd imagine it would involve burning incense or something." He examined the contents of the cupboard. "These are pure products used by a Medicine Man. White Wolf kept this stuff on hand. He had a natural treatment for everything."

A thump overhead startled her. Everyone's focus shot up toward the ceiling. They readied their weapons and crept around the house, keeping their attention overhead.

"A trap door," Rider pointed out.

Shook moved into position. "You may as well come on down. We know you're up there. Don't try anything. We're armed," he called out.

They waited in silence for a few minutes, listening to soft footsteps above.

"Oh no. They must've hidden Rebar's body in the attic. I didn't even know this place had one," she said worriedly.

"Probably just a crawl space," Stoke said.

The little square door finally opened. All three men stood ready and waiting. Two small feet covered in worn blue moccasins appeared first, followed by slender legs then a woman dressed in a blue dress adorned with tan fringe climbed from the opening to the floor and landed with remarkable grace.

They didn't say a word as they stood there staring at her.

Her gaze moved over them intently. "I didn't know who was breaking in," she said, softly, kindly. "Nobody knows of my hiding place. I climb into the rafters to pray."

Cameo gasped as tears sprang to her eyes. "Feather Blue?" This woman looked just like the one in the photos her father had left her.

"Yes," she replied with a warm smile. "You must be Cameo."

"You recognize me?"

"I saw you in the vision. How could my spirit not know my own daughter? I never thought I'd see you again."

Had Jared not left Cameo the video, the letter and the photos, she'd have never known about her real mother or the truth about Malika. She stared at Feather in wonder as emotions surged through her.

Of all the things she expected to find here, her birthmother was not one of them.

"You're my mother . . ." Her cheeks flushed with heat as tears flowed. "You're as beautiful as the photo."

"Shadow Dove," Feather murmured sweetly, then opened her arms. "Forty years I have grieved my twins."

The men lowered their weapons and stood back.

Cameo rushed into her mother's arms and embraced her. They clung to each other. Cameo realized the importance of White Wolf's role in their reunion. He'd given her the Lakota name, and through Shook's vision, Feather had seen her.

The longer they hugged, the more their connection grew. Cameo felt the longing and years of grief melt away in her mother. They wept quietly in a loving embrace for several minutes.

When they pulled back to look at one another, Feather's vivid blue eyes shimmered with emotion. "How did you get into the house?" she asked. "Malika's dreamcatcher has kept outsiders away and me imprisoned since she brought me here."

"Her evil is no match for my Lord," Cameo told her.

Cameo couldn't stop gazing at her beautiful mother. Long ebony hair fell past her shoulders and framed an exquisite face. "Your eyes are extraordinary. I didn't know Native Americans could have blue eyes."

"Normally they don't," Feather said. "I am what white men call a phenomenon, but apparently my people claimed I was born with powerful medicine because blue eyes have never been seen in our nation. White Wolf's father gave me the name *Feather Blue*. He said the heavens gave me my eyes and only birds can soar that high, that I was gifted with grace and vision."

"That is how White Wolf knew of you, and what happened to you."

"Yes. White Wolf's father kept him informed of activity on the reservation after he was forced to leave." Feather looked up at Shook. "He did the right thing, keeping his son and raising him properly. I long to speak with him."

Shook moved to their side. "Are you well enough to travel?"

"Yes. I am not as strong as I should be, but I will get stronger once I'm free of this prison."

"We will take you to my father's cabin where you'll be safe. Then I'm going after Malika. She's wanted by the law."

Feather gazed up at him with sheer affection. "You were also in the vision. You are Tasunke."

He nodded and smiled endearingly at her. "I saw you, too. And this place. But we did not know how to find it. Cameo is actually the reason we were able to find this place. She knew how to use Rebar's tracking."

"The man they shot?" Feather asked.

"You've seen him?" Cameo blurted out.

"He was here. They sent him away."

"Shade and Chamber? They took his body?"

"Took? No, *sent*." Feather tilted her head curiously. "I tended his wound. He did not die. However, the two men you speak of did return. They forced the man named Rebar to make a choice," she said.

"He's alive?" Cameo's eyes widened in shock. "I saw them shoot him."

"I know you did. In my vision, you were running," she replied. "Yes, he is alive and will heal."

Mystified, Cameo asked, "How were we all in Shook's vision together? Can you tell me about it?"

Feather touched her face with a dainty hand. "I am a Medicine Woman. When White Wolf led Shook into the vision quest, he called me, too. The spirits were kind. They allowed me to enter and see my daughter for the first time. Now I understand why because they were leading you to me. Every step taken since that vision has been toward each other." She gazed at Shook. "I'm very proud of you for seeking guidance. You are wise like your father. You must explain the vision to your soulmate."

Shook gave a nod of respect then turned toward Cameo and took her hands in his. "The night you witnessed the shooting was the night I entered a vision quest. The vision consumed me with darkness. It was an unsettling experience. First, a woman came into view. At first I thought it was Malika but as she drew closer, her vivid blue eyes made me realize this was the woman I had seen in your photo. She wore three blue feathers in her hair and was dressed just like her." He gestured toward Feather. "Behind her was a traditional dreamcatcher. Blue feathers floated around her in a haze. She walked toward me down a narrow dirt road bordered on each side by ordinary brown wood frame houses. She stopped a few inches away, a hint of smile on her lips. We stared at each other for a moment before she turned her head and pointed to the right."

Cameo tried to visualize everything he said. "Did you know who she was?"

"Not until I left the vision," he replied then continued, "I saw you running in the dark. You were terrified. Your hair was tangled and your clothes were covered in dirt. I'd never seen you in such a state. I tried to call out to you, but my voice was frozen. The Indian woman then pointed to the left where a man lay on a ratty wooden floor. He wore no shoes or shirt. His jeans were torn and dirty, he lay face down in a heap. The woman went to him and knelt at his side. She touched his face, then eased him onto his back. She nudged him into position and brushed matted hair from his face. Though his eyes were closed there was no mistaking his identity. Dread came over me when I saw blood splattered across Rebar's chest."

"It's like you were there with me," she muttered in awe.

Compassion filled Shook's eyes. "I think I was in a way. The woman looked at me again and spread her arms out to each side. Long fringes draped down from both arms. Her face turned upward, and her lips moved as if praying. Then again, she looked to the right where you were struggling, and back to Rebar on the left. The thought echoed in my brain that Shade finally got his revenge. War on Ricochet has begun. Then I collapsed on the ground beside the fire, panting and soaked in sweat."

Cameo squeezed his hands while watching mixed emotion sweep through his eyes. "I'm sorry you had to live that horror."

"Don't ever be sorry when the spirits grant us wisdom." He placed a tender kiss on her lips. "I worried over why Rebar was in the vision with you."

"You thought I still loved him?"

"Maybe." He shrugged lightly. "But White Wolf told me to

find you, that your heart does not belong to him."

"He's right," she said. "I don't fault you for wondering, though. That's why I went to his place, to gain closure for both of us. But I never expected to witness an attempted murder. Well . . . what at the time I thought was a murder."

"Now I understand the vision," he said. "Everything I saw led us here. And to the truth." He looked at Feather. "You know the truth."

"Yes. Those two men brought Rebar here the night of the vision. They told me to care for him then left. The next day, they returned before I could help the man escape." Feather told them all she'd heard and seen.

"The last piece of my vision." Shook sighed. "Shade is preparing for war just as I thought. He got Rebar and Chamber back into his troop. I'm not surprised by Chamber, but I thought Rebar had more backbone."

"You would've seen him had you arrived sooner. He left with Camille as the sun began to set," Feather said.

"Camille was here?" Cameo gasped in shock.

"Yes, but she did not know me."

"You didn't tell her?"

Feather's expression became like stone. "She had no respect for me. Her interest was only for the man. She disregarded my healing ways. Her mind and heart are not yet open to the truth. I do not speak to rocks."

"Oh . . . I'm sorry. I didn't mean to upset you. I just thought you'd be overjoyed to see your other daughter."

"Joy comes from a bonding of spirits," Feather said. "I pray that Camille will learn to love beyond herself. Perhaps the child in her womb will teach her selflessness."

Cameo's eyes widened. "She really is pregnant? Malika told me she was. Then others said she's not."

"She will enter her third month soon."

"Then she did lie to Rush. That can't be Rush's baby. She

must be carrying Shade's son as Malika said." Cameo felt that familiar knot tightening in her gut.

Feather shook her head. "The man who left with her today is the father."

"Rebar? Camille is pregnant with Rebar's baby? How do you know?"

"I saw it while in prayer."

"Oh my . . . that's the magic Malika has been using. She's been tapping into your spirit to masquerade as you."

Feather nodded. "I'm impressed. Perhaps my medicine has passed down to you. Yes, that is why I am weak and why I take the herbs. Malika has drained my energy for years. The herbs have kept me alive."

Shook gave Cameo an awestruck look. "I'm also impressed. This was the same thought I shared with White Wolf during my last visit. You do have your mother's intuition."

"Thank you," she said softly, humbled by their praise. "I cannot describe my sadness over what they did to you."

Feather reached out and touched her cheek. "Do not feel sorry for me. I chose the wrong path. I didn't know Jared was married until it was too late. I foolishly allowed his charm and wealth to cloud my vision. My reckless actions caused my daughters pain and cast them into a dreadful life. I'm sorry. I hope you can forgive me."

"Of course I forgive you." She hugged her again. "They took advantage of a young girl. I'm amazed that you never gave up all these years."

"My kindhearted, beautiful daughter. I am proud of the woman you've become." Feather brushed tears from her cheeks. "You are the light I've seen in my dreams, the hope that kept me going. You are strong and followed your heart. Your faith led you to an honorable man."

Cameo's mind reeled. The sudden realization that she'd made the right decision in seeking answers dawned on her.

"My intuition served me well, then. My mistake was ignoring the connection I saw between Rebar and Camille in the first place. They really are each other's destiny."

"Sometimes, our journey takes a few turns before we arrive at where we are supposed to be." Feather smiled. "You are with the right man now. Perhaps this Rebar played a role in your path toward Tasunke." She reached out and clasped Shook's wrist with both hands. "Your vision quest is complete. You have the answers you need to move forward." The moment she touched his hand a winding tattoo appeared on his wrist and spiraled upward beneath his leather jacket.

Amazed, Cameo asked, "What is the meaning of this?" She pushed Shook's sleeve up to follow the winding tattoo. "Take your coat off. It doesn't end."

He stared at his arm and slid the jacket off. A fascinating tattoo wound all the way up his arm to his shoulder.

"My gift to you, Tasunke, as a symbol of gratitude for your integrity. The pattern represents your journey." Feather told him. "I am pleased with the union between you and my daughter."

"Thank you," Shook inclined his head slightly then admired his incredible gift. "I'm deeply honored to receive such blessing from my woman's mother."

Rider and Stoke stepped forward to check out Shook's tattooed arm. They marveled over Feather's magical touch.

Feather smiled sweetly and looked from Shook to Cameo. "We have talked much. We should leave before Malika shows up. Surely, she felt something amiss when Cameo broke her spell."

"I agree," Rider spoke up. "We'll put you on with Stoke. He has a bigger passenger seat with a higher backrest. It's a ten-hour ride from here to Pine Ridge."

Feather looked toward a window. "The sun will soon set. You drive at night?"

"We are conditioned to travel any time of day in all weather," Stoke answered her question. "You'll be safe with us."

"Ten hours will be a joy ride after forty years here. I am excited to begin my life. I am afraid to pass by the dreamcatcher, though," Feather admitted with worried eyes.

Cameo walked to the kitchen door, yanked the dreamcatcher off the window and tore it apart with her hands then tossed it in a trashcan near the refrigerator.

"My brain is on overload but I need to get out of here. I want to know everything about you and my ancestry. I still have things that need taken care of. Jared left me something. But all this must wait for now." Cameo reached for Feather's hands. "First, we will take you to Pine Ridge. I can't wait to gather with White Wolf. He will be overjoyed."

Shook pulled his black leather jacket back on and slid an arm around Cameo's waist. "I love how you care about him. I'm looking forward to giving him the good news of our relationship. He will want to celebrate for sure."

"Let's go then." She smiled up at her man. "This is a good day. War will come and we'll be ready. But it won't come today. I long to dance with you again, my love."

"I can't think of a better place to talk than at my father's cabin," Shook said. "We could all use a little downtime. And I'm beginning to feel that waiting for them to make their move may be best."

"Are you thinking he's gonna dig a deeper hole?" Stoke arched his brows curiously.

Shook nodded. "One big enough to bury himself and his witchy cohort in. Malika's got a string of murders on her rap sheet. Shade now has attempted murder and kidnapping. But if he has inherited the General's connections, they'll slip right past the law. That's what I want to prevent."

Rider gave Shook an encouraging slap on the back. "Our

specialty, my friend . . . catching the bad ones outside the law."

"Yep. We best hit the road."

"I need to gather a few things," Feather said, then hurried into the kitchen. She pulled a suede bag from a cupboard and filled it with the herbs and balms Cameo had seen earlier. "These are my medicines." When she finished, she came back to them. "This is all I want to take from this place."

"We can put your satchel in my saddlebag," Stoke told her.

Feather hesitated at the door.

"It's okay." Cameo took her hand and led her out. "Malika has no power over you now and she never will again."

CHAPTER SIX

Sundown — Colorado Springs

"Well, hello, handsome. Welcome home," Malika purred. "Was your excursion a success?"

Shade tossed his jacket on a chair and smiled with confidence. "Indeed, it was. Did you doubt me?"

"I had my concerns. Wasn't sure you had the guts to put a bullet into Rebar. He was your loyal comrade for decades." She curled herself around him seductively. "Did he accept the deal?"

Shade snaked an arm around her slender waist and stared down into mysterious black eyes. "He was putty in my hands once I offered him Camille. Didn't take him long to weigh his options. Chamber was a big help. He made Rebar realize that Ricochet doesn't appreciate him. Of course, Rush moving on Cameo played well for us, too."

"Excellent!" Malika flattened her hands against his chest then slid them over his biceps. "I do have one concern. When Camille showed up for Rebar, I wonder if Feather told her the truth."

"Camille probably wouldn't believe her if she did."

Malika's expression darkened. "The time has come to burn those rundown shacks to the ground and sell the land, before that Indian woman figures out how to contact the girls. They can never know the truth about their past."

Apprehension crept over Shade. "What are you suggesting?"

"I think you know. Feather cannot escape the house. I've kept her bound inside that house and kept my secret involvement with the General and Jared bound inside with her. Jared was going to spill his guts to his daughters, but I stopped him. Your father would've cut a deal and handed me to Shook on a platter had I not stopped him. Shook knows I'm dangerous. He knows too much about me. He's good at his job, I'll give him that. Not once did I feel a hint of suspicion that he's a Fed. And I have never been duped by a man. Now that Feather and Camille have met, Feather is another loose end I need to burn."

"You expect me to burn a house down with her inside?" Shade's gut tensed. "That's another murder to add to your list."

"You shot and kidnapped Rebar. And if Feather gets loose, you can add a second charge of kidnapping to *your* list and attempted murder. You're already in deep. It's only a matter of time before Rebar or Camille tell someone about Feather and it gets back to Cameo. She's nothing like Camille. She'll go on the hunt in search of the truth."

"They can still talk even if we do what you suggest," he pointed out.

"Perhaps. But Camille won't be interested in rumors. She's going to be a mother and set up house with Rebar. And without evidence, Cameo will eventually think they're lying. She doesn't trust them."

Shade noticed a devious glimmer in Malika's eyes. "What are you not telling me? I know you, woman. Don't forget who you're dealing with here."

She averted her gaze and let one finger glide down the center of his chest. "Someday that sharp eye of yours may get you into trouble," she said coyly.

"Mm-hm. Out with it, woman. What's your hidden agenda here?"

"Well . . ." She lifted long dark lashes and looked up without tilting her head. "You know I've been able to use Feather's energy to enhance my own power. She's a legendary Medicine Woman and a phenomenon at that."

"How do you know this?"

"I'm Lakota, too. Have you forgotten? Back when the General first mentioned Jared's new Indian mistress, I checked her out. I knew if I could harness her rare gift, I'd become unstoppable. As you can see, I succeeded."

He sighed with pointed brows. "You are something else, that's for sure. How'd you know what to do?"

"My biggest coup was taking her babies. They contained her lifeforce. Raising them as my own gave me what I needed. Then I split them up so they could never use their twin bond against me."

"Okay . . . so you have Feather's power. Won't you lose it if you kill her?"

A wicked grin curved Malika's red-painted lips. "Now that she's met her daughter, her Medicine is stronger than ever. By burning the house down with her inside and still under my control, all that power will be mine forever."

Shade gave her a cockeyed look. "You're crazy, ya know that? I don't believe any of this witchy voodoo BS. But you are an insatiable vamp that I want in my bed. I'm not into killing people, though."

"If we don't cut this off at the pass, you will be sorry, Shade. Mark my words. If Cameo gets wind that Feather is alive, she'll stop at nothing to find her just like she did everything in her power to rescue me thinking that I'm her mother. That girl is tenacious and now she's got her Fed boyfriend helping her. Another reason I need to eliminate him. I just can't figure out how. He's smart . . . too smart."

"Hey, we have some brains on our side, now. Rebar's a genius. Talon and Kohl, too."

Malika scoffed. "With gadgets, yes. But are they attorneys? Because that's what you'll need if we don't stop Ricochet."

"I could've stopped Ricochet weeks ago if not for those problematic twins. We finally got Camille out. How do we get Cameo?"

"By taking out Shook. He's most likely looking for me. He doesn't know I'm more powerful than ever. That man is in for an awakening. I'll handle him. You get rid of the Medicine Woman. Then Ricochet will be nothing more than a handful of nobodies. I'll have both my daughters together and the power of Feather Blue."

"They aren't your daughters," he reminded her.

She glared at him. "They *are* my daughters. I cared for them since the day they were born. Feather may have carried them, but I've always considered them mine from the day we found out she was pregnant. That's why we took Feather into hiding before she gave birth. She never held them or laid eyes upon them. Camille and Cameo are *my* twins. Don't ever forget that. Another reason we must get rid of Feather."

Shade didn't like this plan at all. He could see numerous flaws and ways it could go wrong. He wasn't a killer. He accomplished what he set out to do, teach Rebar a lesson, steal him and Camille from Ricochet, and show the weak biker group who had more clout.

He wasn't onboard with going after an FBI agent or killing an innocent woman. His lust for Malika had led him into unchartered territory. He wondered how he'd drifted this far from the man he used to be.

When he first hooked up with Malika, he didn't know about Feather. The Medicine Woman was part of Malika's past with his father, the General. They'd done a good job of keeping their secret, including killing Jared when he was about to talk.

Since learning about Feather and his father's sordid past,

Shade felt in over his head at times. Along with inheriting the General's massive wealth and influential contacts, he seemed to have taken on the fallout of his illegal dealings as well. Being the new kingpin didn't always feel as good as he thought it would.

There were days when he missed hanging out with his men and doing what they'd always done best, complete top secret military assignments. However, those days seemed gone now.

"C'mon, stud." She took his hand. "Take me upstairs to celebrate our victory."

Shade let her lead him up the winding staircase, but he didn't feel much like celebrating. Bringing Rebar, Chamber, Talon, and Kohl back to his troop felt right. And Camille finding happiness with Rebar was a bonus, a relief from his guilt over cheating on her. She and Rebar had connected from the moment they met. Rebar comforted her in ways Shade never could.

He understood Malika's desire to pull Cameo out of Ricochet. However, their initial plan never involved coldblooded murder. They'd schemed to destroy Ricochet, and Shade felt they'd delivered a significant blow. He'd achieved his goal of retrieving his men and getting Camille out of the way so he could have his troop back together and Malika in his bed fulltime.

Her chatter about Indian medicine and strange power disturbed him. He hadn't considered the dark past she shared with his father and Jared before pursuing her. He only knew that he wanted her. She was the most mysteriously alluring female he'd ever met, and now she was his.

"You're suddenly quiet," she said upon stretching across his king bed. "You better not be getting soft on me." She narrowed her eyes. "You're not attracted to that Indian woman, are you?"

"No. Not at all." He pulled off his clothes. "Just mulling things over."

"There's nothing to mull. We get rid of Feather and Shook. Then we'll decide what to do with the rest of Ricochet. I don't need more of those men getting in my way."

"In your way of what?"

She furrowed her brows at him. "My rise to power. With your wealth and contacts, we can rebuild that shameful stretch of housing your father used for his business."

"Or like you said, sell the land. I'm not worried about that slum. I plan to sell it to the highest bidder."

"That land is perfect for running a stable. It just needs to be updated. Well, gutted and rebuilt in this case."

Shade gave her a pointed look. "Stable? Are you getting into horses or something?"

She laughed mockingly. "Shade, you're such a kidder. A brothel, my darling man. I've always wanted to be in a position over others. Growing up on the rez was humiliating. I swore I'd pull myself up and become envied, like Feather Blue."

"Running a whorehouse isn't going to gain you respect."

"Not a whorehouse but an escort service where the women can live under my care, and men will have to pay top dollar for our services. Men think they can simply take what they want and go on their way. I will teach my girls how to control them, make them beg. And any man that steps out of line or hurts one of my girls will answer to me." She ran one hand down her shapely leg while gazing up at him. "You of all people, should know what that entails."

His brows shot up. "I thought you wanted to move in with me, settle down and live a good life together."

"Yes, I do. But I have ambitions. Do you expect me to lie around and wait for you to come home after you're done running about with your comrades? I'm your woman, Shade. But don't try to keep me on a leash. Now come to bed and make me feel like your woman. I'm tired of talking."

He eased onto the bed, searching her eyes for a sign of warmth or jest but saw only ice. She was serious about her goals. He couldn't fathom why she wanted to run an escort service.

Was she out to take revenge on the entire male race? Why did she harbor this intense animosity toward them? She had a dark need to control men, except for him. She satisfied him in every way. He'd never detected a hint of resistance in her.

He thought about her vendetta toward Shook. The man had bedded her while undercover to gain access to her secrets. His betrayal cut her deeply, this Shade knew. He worried how far she'd go to exact her revenge on the man. She'd already shown she wasn't above killing any man who crossed her.

Shade began to worry. Malika had clearly stated she wanted his wealth. In return, she was the most agreeable woman in bed he'd ever known. If he dared to thwart her plans, he'd become her next target.

If this stunning vixen possessed the skill and chutzpah to kill a congressman, a General, and target a Federal Agent, Shade realized she'd have no problem offing him if he posed a threat to her agenda. He began to understand how his father and Jared fell into her web.

He forced his worry aside in order to please her. She seemed agitated and the last thing he wanted was to escalate her troubled thoughts. She'd waited patiently for him to return from his mission. The least he could do was make her happy to see him again. This was one woman he'd have to tread lightly around.

CHAPTER SEVEN

Pine Ridge

An enchanting sunrise greeted them as they pulled up to White Wolf's cabin. Shook, Rider, and Stoke had ridden straight through all night with only stops for snacks and restroom breaks. She'd never ridden so hard.

Cameo stifled a yawn while gazing at the vivid shades of gold, blue, and pink lacing the eastern Dakota horizon. The reality that her future home was in this beautiful state still hadn't registered fully in her mind. And she still needed to visit the bank and claim her land. She now trusted Shook enough to tell him. However, other matters would come first. Feather was free and tonight they'd celebrate with a fire and most likely, roasted food.

White Wolf peeked out from his cabin as the Harleys rumbled to a halt. A big grin spread to his eyes as he ambled toward them. His eyes widened upon spotting their new passenger.

"Feather Blue!" He took her hands and helped her off Stoke's bike. "What a great day this is. My father would be overjoyed to see your return."

"White Wolf . . ." She kissed his cheek. "It is good to see you. Your father was dear to me."

"Cloud Walking grieved when you disappeared. Come, let us sit and eat. Perhaps you will tell us about your journey. I've seen many confusing visions concerning you."

Cameo waited for the guys to secure their bikes. She

watched Feather stroll to the fire with White Wolf. They looked adorable together. Fortunately, they were only friends. She'd be heartbroken if she and Shook had somehow been related. By the light in White Wolf's eyes, she considered they may have joined in marriage had Feather not hooked up with Jared. Then again, her life would've been entirely different if her mother had chosen a different man.

She watched Shook inspect his bike from end to end. His attention to detail impressed her. She felt safe riding with a man who made sure the vehicle was well maintained. His hair was getting longer. He looked hot in the black riding leathers with that layered straight black hair hanging a few inches past the collar now. She wondered if he'd continue to let it grow long.

He glanced over and caught her gawking. Her cheeks flushed. She averted her eyes and pretended to be casually staring into the distance. After finishing up at the bike he came to her side, a hint of a grin on his face.

"I love when I catch you gazing at me the way you do when you think I'm not aware," he softly teased, taking her into his arms.

She looked up into his eyes. "I get lost in you."

"Mm. Kimimila, you turn me on." He nuzzled her ear.

"Likewise, my handsome warrior."

Their lips met in a deeply affectionate kiss laced with heat. As tired as she was, Cameo could still see herself going a round or two with this irresistible man. She eased from the kiss.

"We better stop before I can't," she whispered.

He gave her a wink that stirred flutters down low. "Tonight, my love, when all is quiet, we'll find a private place to lay our blanket."

"I should take a nap then," she said with a playful smile.

"Let's join the others. You can lean on me and rest. Are you hungry?"

"Depends on what you're offering," she teased.

He laughed a little. "You are in a rambunctious mood."

"Ten hours, snuggled behind you, feeling your hair against my face and smelling your stimulating scent . . . yeah, just a little."

"Well . . ." He laughed again. "I promise to take care of you. But for now, how about this?" He pulled a chocolate bar from his jacket pocket. "I picked it up for you at one of our stops for fuel. I know you're not fond of White Wolf's cooking, so I brought snacks."

"You're a sweetheart." She accepted the chocolate and unwrapped it, then offered him a bite. They shared the delicious treat while wandering over to the circle.

Rider and Stoke had already plopped onto the grass. White Wolf also sat on the grass instead of his tree stump this time. Cameo figured his change in routine had a lot to do with the beautiful Feather Blue who sat cross-legged on the brown grass between White Wolf and Stoke.

"White Wolf, you've abandoned your stump." She couldn't resist needling him.

"Feather speaks softly," he said. "I don't want to miss a word she says."

"Nice save," Cameo countered with a grin.

His black eyes glimmered playfully. "It is good to see you with my son. Does this mean you have found your heart, Shadow Dove? When we last visited, you seemed lost."

"I'm no longer lost," she replied. "Shook and I have conquered the obstacles that were in our way."

"Very good news." He nodded in approval. "We have much to celebrate. My son has found his soulmate at last, and the mystery of Feather Blue has been solved."

Shook found a soft patch of grass to sit on. He pulled Cameo onto his lap, wrapped both arms around her waist from behind and rested his chin on her shoulder. She sunk into his embrace, leaning her head back against him.

"This feels so good." She sighed.

He kissed her neck. "For sure."

They listened as White Wolf asked Feather to share her story. He filled a long pipe with tobacco and passed it around. Shook took one short puff to appease his father but no more. Cameo didn't like the taste, so she passed.

Feather seemed totally composed while she spoke, as if she'd never endured trauma or captivity. She accepted the pipe, which surprised Cameo. This was where she'd get to know her birthmother for the first time.

She told them much of what Cameo had heard, but it felt better hearing the facts from the woman who knew them firsthand and spoke the entire truth. Cameo had fulfilled Jared's wishes by finding Feather and bringing her safely away from Malika.

Now Shook could bring the criminals to justice in whatever manner he saw fit. Even Rebar had stepped out of the way and took Camilla with him.

Though she shouldn't be, Cameo was shocked at how easily Rebar had taken her back. She'd been right all along about those two. Even so, her involvement led her to a man she admired, respected, fiercely loved, and even trusted. By her standards, men didn't get any better than Shook.

"I am curious . . . Mother . . ." She felt awkward calling her that. "How did you end up working for Jared?" Cameo asked during a lull in conversation.

"I took jobs off the reservation to earn money for college. One of those jobs was as a secretary for Jared. It was only supposed to be temporary, but he hired me as his personal assistant. I couldn't turn down his offer. What I earned working for him more than met my needs and helped my parents. At first, Ina and Até liked Jared very much. They were proud that their only child had achieved such success. However, all that changed when we learned he had a wife and four sons." A faraway expression shadowed her face for an instant. "I told him we could no longer date, that I would not dishonor my family by continuing to see him. He refused to accept my decision. That night, after work, he grabbed me before I left the office. The General was waiting in a big black car. They bound me with rope and took me into hiding with Malika. Jared knew everything yet did nothing. He was a spineless lizard. I was young and gullible."

Cameo fought back tears and swallowed her rage. "Jared abducted you?"

Feather nodded once. "The three of them used me as a surrogate for Malika. Jared did his part by getting me pregnant. He bowed to the General's every command."

"He told quite a different story on the video. It bore similarities but he made himself look like a victim."

"Of course he would." Feather scowled. "He was a politician. His tongue knows how to twist the truth like a snake in the grass."

"He left me your photo, and a letter asking me to find you and care for you. But I had no idea he took part in their crime," she told Feather. "He said you were the love of his life."

"He doesn't know the meaning of love," she responded in a flat tone. "Still, I'm glad he told at least one truth, that I am your mother. My prayers have been answered. I'm with my daughter."

"But not—" Cameo frowned.

"In time, my brave one. Camille's faith presently lies elsewhere. We must find a way to meet her where her mind is." Feather's patience was astounding.

White Wolf cleared his throat to speak. "We now know the whole truth at last. My heart is sad for the pain you endured, yet my spirit rejoices that you survived and have come home," he told her, affection in his voice. "Shadow Dove has destroyed Malika's hold over you. Your medicine will return, and you will yet again become legendary. Our people will want to know that you've been found."

"Thank you, my friend," Feather responded sweetly. "Many moons have passed, and the new generation is more interested in modern ways. It is good enough that I'm free and have my daughter. Even better, that she is with your son. I could not hope for a more suitable match."

Cameo glanced up at Shook and smiled. He returned her smile and kissed her lips. Though they weren't that young, she felt younger than ever, and Shook didn't look anywhere close to fifty. He'd obviously taken great care of himself. Or maybe it was his strong Lakota genetics that made him so utterly irresistible and virile at his age.

Either way, she didn't care that it took so long to find each other. He was more than worth the wait. She looked forward to dancing with him tonight in the firelight with the flames emulating their dance.

Feather seemed strong. After all she'd been through, she still looked radiant and full of life. She was absolutely beautiful. Cameo watched her mother chat amiably with White Wolf. They talked about old ways, and she had a lot of questions about people Cameo didn't know, people who'd lived on the reservation that Feather never got to see again. White Wolf graciously filled her in on the life she'd missed.

Their conversation gradually flowed to less intense subjects such as medicine, which they both practiced. They talked about various remedies and traditions, and ancient Lakota creeds.

Feather told them how she used natural tonics to rejuvenate her mind and body after Malika's unorthodox spells. She called Malika a *trickster*—one who exhibits great intellect or secret knowledge and uses it to defy conventional behavior.

Listening to her mother was fascinating although bitter-sweet. Feather had missed forty years of her life at the hands of Malika Rain and two evil men, one of whom was her father. Though relieved that Feather was now free, Cameo loathed Jared for what he'd done, and for the lies he left amidst a smattering of truth. He was indeed a coward, and she was glad she didn't have to meet him.

Only one of Feather's abductors remained. Cameo looked forward to the day when Shook cuffed Malika and hauled her off to prison. She was long overdue in paying for her crimes.

"What were my grandparents like?" Cameo asked, hoping her mother wouldn't mind reminiscing. "What was your life like before you met Jared?"

She smiled graciously. Warmth shimmered in her eyes. "We were poor. All families on the reservation lived in poverty. But we preserved our customs and beliefs. My father was called Hungry Bear because he was a big man with an even bigger appetite." She laughed a little. Her laugh was as dainty as her appearance. "My mother was known as Summer Dove because she was born on the seventh moon and possessed beauty, grace, and could sing like a bird. She was patient and kind yet strong. You remind me of her. I see the same spirit in your eyes I saw in hers."

"White Wolf gave me the name Shadow Dove. He said I am the Shadow of Feather Blue and carry the spirit of my mother. I was always troubled by this because I thought Malika was my mother."

White Wolf nodded. "I received the name in prayer for Feather."

"It's perfect," Feather said. "I was also born on the seventh moon. She didn't have your beautiful blonde hair, though. I'm afraid you got that from your father's side. I think in a way, Jared was torn between worlds. He wanted to fit into mine but was bound in his. The General had taken control of him years before we met. It seems that Malika dictated both men's actions. She had an uncanny influence over men."

"She still does." Cameo scowled. "The General's son, Shade, is her newest conquest."

"Yes. I sensed that when we met. He seemed submissive to her."

"Did you have a happy childhood?"

"We made the best of it. When the Native American teachers noticed how well I did with my lessons, they approached my parents about sending me to the white man's school. I was terrified. But mother wanted the best for me. She worked hard making beautiful garments and jewelry to sell. Father made wooden flutes, as many of the men did. They wanted me to live a better life. They used their money to buy me modern clothes so I'd fit into the outside world." Feather sighed despondently. "I let them down. My involvement with Jared ended all their hopes for me and all the dreams I had for myself. Pregnant at sixteen to a married man was a disgrace."

"You were trying to get out of poverty and became the victim of an evil plot," Cameo said.

She couldn't begin to sort the ladder of lies that had been dropped into her life since she'd met Malika. Her thoughts whipped back to their confrontation with the General the day he was killed. The argument between him and Malika made it seem like Malika had actually been pregnant. And White Wolf knew Feather was pregnant before she left the reservation. She did a quick calculation. Five people all had a different account of Feather's life story.

First Malika, then the General, White Wolf, Jared, and now Feather herself had all revealed their version of Cameo and Camille's broken lives. She began to understand why Camille didn't want any part of this. The adults in their lives had made a mess. Even Shook's father took the wayward path.

She stared at her mother, wondering how to feel.

"I wish I had stayed on the reservation and married a man from our tribe," Feather said. "Many young warriors had their eyes on me. However, my parents wanted me to marry a wealthy man, not a poor boy on the rez."

"Did you and White Wolf grow up together?"

"Not really. I was only seven when he left to raise Tasunke. He was twenty-seven. I spent more time with his father than I did with him."

Cameo turned her attention toward White Wolf. "I thought you were a wild young warrior when you met Rain Song."

He shrugged with a silly grin. "I felt young. Look at Tasunke! Fifty and just found his love."

"Age seems to trouble you," Feather commented.

"No. I'm just trying to wrap my mind around all the details of my past."

"Don't worry over the past, child. You have a bright future to think about. White Wolf is twenty years older than I am. Most of what we know about each other was exchanged by his father. As Chief Medicine Man, Cloud Walking knew everyone, and all the people sought his wisdom at one time or another. He was a good listener." Feather became suddenly uneasy. "Excuse me, please. I'll be right back." She got to her feet and disappeared into the cabin.

Cameo caught Shook's perplexed expression. Hair on her arms bristled. Something compelled her to turn toward the bikes.

"Did you really believe you could hide Feather from me?" Malika stood at the edge of the clearing, her raven hair blowing in the mountain breeze. A fringed white dress clung to her curvy figure and matching moccasins adorned her feet. "Feather belongs to me. I came to take her home."

Shook, Rider, and Stoke leapt to their feet but none were armed. They'd left their firearms and jackets on the bikes.

Malika's gaze went to Shook. "My, my, you look so fine.

My daughter has very good taste in men."

"She's not your daughter, and you're crazy to show up here. You know we have to take you into custody," Shook responded much calmer than Cameo felt.

"Shook, you gorgeous stud, you have to catch me first." Malika's eyes narrowed and her mood darkened. "You tricked me, betrayed me, and now threaten to haul me off to prison. You have no idea who you're dealing with. Then again, maybe you do."

"Where's your partner in crime hiding?" he asked and gave Rider and Stoke a nod. They scouted the wood line.

"Shade's not here. Seems he has an aversion to tangling with an FBI man."

Cameo was baffled over how Malika had traveled all the way from Amarillo to Pine Ridge without help. She no longer possessed Feather's power. If Shade hadn't driven her, who had? She knew Rebar wouldn't, and she doubted that Camille would . . . or would she? Would her twin commit the ultimate betrayal and bring the she-devil here to cause trouble? After all, Camille still thought the woman was her mother. They had bonded somehow—a disturbing thought.

"Give it up, Malika. It's only a matter of time before we reign you back in," Shook snapped.

Cameo couldn't fathom how he kept his wit in the face of evil. Every nerve in her body was on guard.

"No, darling. You have the facts all wrong. And you picked the wrong woman to scorn."

Without warning, Shook threw Cameo to the ground and covered her body with his. She heard several soft whooshes overhead. A few seconds later, he cautiously lifted his head, then stood and lifted Cameo to her feet.

She gasped at the sight of Malika slumping over Rider's Harley. Six arrows protruded from her back.

CHAPTER EIGHT

A*rrows?* Cameo heard soft footsteps approach then saw Feather march past them with a bow in one hand. She grabbed Malika by the hair and whipped her lifeless body to the ground.

Shook glanced at Cameo. "Are you okay, babe?"

"Yeah . . . kind of a déjà vu." A flashback of when she'd fired arrows into Joan while held prisoner with Rush came over her. "Guess I have more of my mother in me than I realized."

Everyone edged over to where Feather stood over Malika who lay on the ground with a gun in one hand.

"How'd you know?" Shook asked her.

Feather met his gaze straight on. "I felt her trying to pull energy from me. Then I saw her in my mind coming up the path with a gun hidden in her hand. She was planning to fulfill her vendetta against Shook. She called on the dark spirits to fuel her rage and hate."

"I can't believe she was going to shoot him in broad daylight in front of witnesses." Cameo stared at the body in horror.

"She thought she'd use her blue smoke trick to vanish. Her mistake was trying to channel from me. She didn't expect me to feel it. Malika underestimated my medicine."

Cameo murmured a humble prayer of thanks to God for Feather's insight and quick thinking. Though she didn't completely believe in the Native American religion or their unconventional medicine, she'd never disrespect their beliefs.

"Does this mean the war against Ricochet is over?" Cameo looked from Shook to Rider to Stoke.

"I'd say it just escalated," Stoke replied. "Someone drove her up here to make a deliberate attempt on Shook's life."

"But who would do that?"

"Let's see if we can find out." Stoke motioned to Rider and the two men sprinted toward the path leading down to the road.

Feather looked up at Shook. "I guess you have to take me into custody. It's worth it to get rid of her."

"Custody for what?" asked Shook. "Self-defense? Besides, I didn't see a thing." He turned toward his father. "Did you see anything, Até?"

"Just a wild animal in the brush," White Wolf replied then wandered back to the cabin and began packing his pipe.

Shook led Cameo to the firepit. "We should leave tonight. I know you're exhausted. But I can't be around to see what they do with her body." Conflict weighed his voice.

"What body?" Feather asked upon following them.

Cameo looked toward the bikes at the same time Shook did. Everything appeared normal. There wasn't a trace of Malika.

"What did you do, Mother?"

"Cloud Walking taught me much," she said nonchalantly, yet an air of mystery surrounded her. "We spent many hours together because he knew of my gift and wanted to perfect it. Though he was much older, he was fond of me. He showed me how to use the bow and arrow, how to hunt and fish. I think he enjoyed having another student because his son was grown. I learned all my medicine from him."

"You are a fascinating woman, Mother." Cameo gazed at her in awe. She'd just fired arrows into Malika and saved Shook's life, yet she was utterly composed. She began to realize that her mother was more of a phenomenon than anyone thought.

Perhaps the legend of Feather Blue entails stories untold.

Feather reached out and touched her arm. Her touch felt unusually warm. "We are not so different, Shadow Dove. I understand that you must leave for now. I'll stay here with White Wolf."

"That's probably a good idea," Shook agreed. "Clearly, you and my father are capable of defending yourselves. I don't think Shade and his troop will be after you anyway. They want Ricochet out of the way."

"What is Ricochet?" Feather asked.

"The good guys." Shook studied her face for a moment then walked away.

Stoke and Rider jogged over to them. With a mere glance, Shook seemed to communicate their departure with them before he walked to White Wolf and bid him farewell.

He clasped forearms with his father. "I'm sorry we cannot stay to celebrate. There are matters I must take care of."

White Wolf nodded knowingly. "Be safe, my son. Return when your war is won."

"We will see you again," Shook said, then looked at Feather. "I'm not exactly sure what happened here, but I thank you for saving me from Malika's ambush. You will be safe with my father."

Feather smiled. "One good turn deserves another. Thank you for freeing me and reuniting me with Shadow Dove."

Cameo hugged Feather. "I hope to see you again soon. Maybe we'll receive a miracle and Camille will come to her senses."

"Focus on your future with Tasunke. He is worthy of your heart," Feather told her.

Cameo slanted a puzzled look over her mother's dismissal of Camille. But she didn't want to press. Feather had just escaped a hellish existence and needed time to heal.

"I will. I have things that need taken care of so I'm not sure when I'll get back up here. I wish we'd had a longer visit."

"We have plenty of time. Now go. Your man looks rest-less."

Cameo nodded then walked with Shook to the bikes where Stoke and Rider waited. She scanned the area, visually scouring the ground for signs of Malika. Not a trace of evidence remained, not even a patch of flattened grass.

"Do any of you think this is strange?" she asked the guys.

They nodded. "Seems to be a pattern of missing bodies lately," Rider pointed out.

Shook examined the area as well, a baffled look on his face. He finally gave up and looked at his friends. "Did you find any leads?"

Rider nodded. "There was a car waiting at the road when we got down there. I think it was waiting for Malika. When the driver spotted us, it took off. We didn't get a look at who was in the car, though."

"Did you get a make on the car?" Shook pried.

Stoke flicked a spent cigarette to the ground and stomped it with his boot then replied, "Yeah . . . a black Hemi Cuda."

Chamber? She didn't need to say what everyone was thinking.

Cameo leaned into Shook as he slid an arm around her waist. He'd been pensive since the encounter with Malika. She knew the entire incident troubled him more than he wanted to admit.

"Seems that Shade and his henchmen are out to settle the score over our bust on the General," Shook said. "I'm not even sure what I saw at the cabin was real." He raked a hand through his long black hair. "Let's get out of this area and find a hotel for the night. We're all in need of sleep."

"I know of a place we can go where no one will find us." Cameo decided the time had come to trust her man and his two closest friends with the one thing she hadn't revealed to anyone yet. "We need a place to clear our heads."

The three men looked at her with marked interest. She rooted through her bag to the concealed zippered pouch and pulled out an envelope.

"I don't know where this is. I haven't had time to GPS it. So I'm hoping it's not too far away." She handed Shook the handwritten letter left to her by Jared.

"What's this?" His eyes met hers.

"The last piece of the puzzle to my past. I'm sorry I didn't show it to you the night you watched the DVD, but I wasn't sure who to trust."

His expression softened and he looked at her as only he could do. "No explanation needed, my love. You had every reason to hold back." He read the letter. "Wow . . . this is incredible."

"Is it far from here?" she asked.

"Only an hour's drive. Are you sure about this?"

She nodded. "I want to help. The three of you are the only people I trust right now."

Shook turned toward their friends. "Jared left her two-hundred acres in Shep's Canyon, Hot Springs. Think you can push through a bit longer?"

"You know us." Rider scoffed. "We've gone days without sleep on some assignments. It's what we do."

Stoke gave Cameo an approving nod. "Thanks for trusting us. That is one righteous inheritance."

"Righteous?" She gave him a quirky look.

"Ah, just my way of saying something's fantastic."

She smiled at his lighter side. "I know nothing about land in South Dakota. This wasn't one of the states I considered settling in when I returned to America. Do you think it's a nice piece of property?"

"Paradise on earth," Rider said. "Jared definitely wanted to make things right with you."

She offered him a grateful smile. "Thank you for that. It's been difficult hearing how bad he was."

Shook wrapped her in a comforting hug. "He made one huge mistake that ruined the rest of his life, he trusted the General. I've listened and watched and still don't know whose story to believe. But the DVD showed how afraid he was. And this letter proves how much he loved you. Try to focus on this. Because this is the most upright thing the man ever did, and he did it for you."

Her gaze moved around their tight circle. "You all are awesome. I want to believe that part of my past had something good in it. I truly appreciate your optimism."

"Hey, we've been around. We gotta look at the half-full glass in our line of work. Keeps us sane." Stoke chuckled. "Well, almost sane."

"Looks like our main man here will be moving north, eh buddy?" Rider gave Shook a friendly slap on the back.

"That's up to my pretty lady, here," Shook replied.

Cameo looked up at him as he held her affectionately. "You'd leave Texas?"

"Baby, I'd follow you to Timbuktu if you asked me to." He dropped a quick kiss on her lips.

"I see Sturgis in our future," Rider teased.

Stoke's eyes brightened. "Hell yeah. We're only a stone's throw away up here. That is, if Halo doesn't mind us hanging out now and then."

"Are you kidding? I'd love the company. Maybe you can bring your girlfriends up and camp. Surely, there's enough room on my land for all of us. It's still early in the day. Can we swing by this bank he listed and claim my land?"

"We would love that. You are one fine, generous lady," Rider told her. "I knew you were the right woman for our man Shook."

"You seem very close to each other," she noted.

"Yeah," Shook said. "Fifteen years together in the Bureau. When your life depends on your partners, you develop deep trust."

"Are you looking to retire soon?" Stoke arched questioning brows.

"I've given it a lot of thought lately." Shook glanced adoringly at Cameo. "Yeah . . . this is my last assignment."

"We're gonna miss ya, but you've put in more than enough time. Actually, I'm impressed you didn't burn out before the twenty," Rider said.

"I probably would have if not for the two best partners a man could ask for. Just because I'm leaving the force, don't stop coming around," Shook told them. "I always knew that if I found the right woman, I'd retire. I never wanted my lady to be stuck with an absentee man."

Rider half nodded, half shrugged. "We've got five years to go. Won't be the same without you but I totally get where you're coming from."

Shook subtly glanced over at White Wolf and Feather. Cameo studied his expression. She'd never seen him rattled but something had spooked him over their recent encounter with Malika.

"Are you okay, baby?" she murmured.

"Hm?" He turned his attention back toward her. "Yeah . . . just tired. Let's get out of here."

From the corner of her eye, she caught Rider and Stoke exchange wary looks. Something definitely had these guys concerned. In all the time she'd spent with them, at Raton, Amarillo, and on Rush's ranch, they'd always been calm, cool and collected. She didn't think anything could shake them.

Today they'd all witnessed an unexpected confrontation between two powerful women. She had to admit to herself, nothing about it seemed real. She'd only known her mother for little over a day and already an uncanny aura emanated from her. Cameo wondered if her life would ever feel normal again.

"I'm up for that," she said quietly. "Let's get out of here."

Stoke and Rider straddled their bikes.

Shook pulled Cameo into his arms and buried his face against her neck. He wrapped himself around her in an embrace laden with need. She stroked his sleek hair and clung to him, extending all her love, sensing his distress.

"I feel it, too, my love," she whispered next to his ear.

"Kimimila . . . please don't ever leave me."

"I'd never leave you, baby. Why would you say that?"

"White Wolf told me that I'm susceptible to the dark world until the vision quest is resolved. I felt it that night Malika tried pulling you away. Then again on the night of vision quest. White Wolf told me not to fight it." He lifted his head so that their eyes met, his carried an emotion she'd never seen in him—fear. "I'm not sure I like my father's world. So much darkness, butterfly . . . darkness as I've never felt before."

"Yes, I thought it was just me. We will fight it together."

"Everything about this mission has gone against my principles."

She caressed his cheek while gazing back at him, pained by his anguish. "Mine, too. I didn't want to voice my thoughts, though, for fear of offending you. You seemed so comfortable in White Wolf's world."

"Trick of the trade," he confessed. "Masking my feelings. Except when it comes to you. My love for you is the first real thing I've ever felt. I'm afraid this darkness will push you away."

"I'm not afraid of storms, no matter how dark they get."

"I don't fear the storm, or the darkness . . . only that it would drive away the best gift I ever received. You. I can handle anything . . ." He framed her face between gentle hands. "But I would not survive losing you."

She slid her hands into his hair. They stood with their faces so close she could feel his warm breath feather her lips. "I love you, Shook, more than I've ever loved anyone. You made me wait when I didn't want to. You've been strong when I was falling apart. Your self-control pushed me to face my past and conquer it. You are everything I need *and* everything I want."

He smiled tenderly at her remark. She knew he recalled what he'd asked her that first night together in the hotel. Relief swept through the depth of his engaging eyes.

"I love you, my precious Halo." He hugged her again, bathing her in intense affection. Never had anyone held her like this. His heart was so pure, so true. Tears misted her eyes as they clung to each other one more time before taking to the road. "You are my light in this darkness."

His candor touched her. All these weeks he'd been a pillar of restraint and stoicism. This man—this incredible, upright, strong, gorgeous male chose her to love and trust. She sensed the road before them entailed mountains to move, but she'd never felt more passionate about anything than taking this journey with him.

"Whatever we face, don't ever let go of us," she murmured.

He brushed a sweet kiss over her lips then drew her into his heart with those make love to me eyes. "Never, my love. Never."

Read what happens next in Feather Blue: Book 11

About the Author

Shiloh is a bookworm who grew into an author. Writing has been a way of life for her since grade school. In her words, "The only time I'm truly free is when I'm writing."

As a survivor of hardship and chronic disease, she takes one day at a time and treasures the simple things in life. Shiloh is a Christian, loves animals and practices being kind and generous every day.

Her achievements include The Golden Wings Award for her debut novel The Satellite, the UK Nobel Pin and Editor's Choice Award for her poem The Lonely Man, numerous 5 Star Reviews from Fallen Angels Reviews, InD'tale Magazine, and other professional reviewers for novels published under former pen names.

Her novel Forever in Darkness became a finalist in the 2017 RONE Awards.

Her novel *Chained Reaction* earned her third 5 Star Crowned Heart Review and a nomination for the RONE 2021 Awards.

Writing stories you'll live in!

www.SusanZoeBella.com

www.ingramcontent.com/pod-product-compliance
Lightning Source LLC
Chambersburg PA
CBHW070522130626
46555CB00003B/1312